CHANCE OF ROMANCE

KYLIE GILMORE

Cover design by Sweet 'N Spicy Designs

Published by: Extra Fancy Books

ISBN-13: 978-1-942238-39-3

Because a romance book club would rock…

1

"I'm not going to lie to America, Hailey!" Sabrina Clarke exclaimed.

Hailey, leader of the Happy Endings Book Club and a die-hard romantic, leaned forward. "There's absolutely nothing wrong with a fake engagement!"

Sabrina threw her hands up. "In a book, yes. In reality, no." That was the makings of a romance novel—perfect for their romance book club, crazy in real life. And it certainly wouldn't solve her problem.

Sabrina's article, "Goodbye Commitment-Phobe, Hello Happiness!" had published last week on the popular Sugar Buzz blog. Alarming things had been happening ever since. First, the post had gone viral. She'd nearly had a heart attack when the editor emailed to tell her it had a million views and was still going strong. And then today Sabrina got a call inviting her for an interview on *Sunshine America,* a national morning talk show dedicated to good news. She'd hyperventilated and told them she'd have to check her schedule and get back to them. She was a relationship counselor with a thriving practice, and it was *everything* to her.

She'd been fretting over her decision ever since, which was why she'd told her friends of her dilemma the moment they sat down at book club. She wanted to help a broader audience, but she feared public scrutiny would reveal the truth—she was a complete fraud. Here she was, a relationship counselor, and she didn't have a committed relationship of her own. That was when the fake fiancé came up, a fanciful notion born of their love of romance novels.

Her friends—every last one of the eight women seated in a circle at Something's Brewing Café—erupted in support of the fake fiancé. Not happening. She prided herself on being honest.

Sabrina pushed her long dirty-blond hair behind her ears, caught herself mid-eyeroll, and quickly looked to the ceiling. The golden light of the hanging sconces set a pretty glow up there, the shadows peculiarly phallic. She looked away, focusing on the baked-goods counter and telling herself that just because it had been a while didn't mean she was desperate. Her eye caught on the phallic éclairs. The symbolism was not lost on her. It was getting worse by the week and really starting to get to her. Hormones? Her friends all finding their forever loves? Her secret lust for her one and only guy friend? Probably all of the above. Well, a fake fiancé wouldn't fix that either.

Lexi's voice cut through the chatter. She was a close friend, a brunette with almond-shaped brown eyes and a practical, no-nonsense manner. "Let's look at the facts. Number one, Sabrina is no longer just a relationship healer for Clover Park, now she's a relationship healer for all of America."

"Not true," Sabrina protested. She'd had a feature article in *The Clover Park Record* that called her a relationship healer, but that was it. No one had said she was a healer beyond that.

Lexi went on as if Sabrina hadn't spoken. "Fact number two! The entire country is buzzing about your article! By the way, that title was genius click bait. Are you sure you don't have PR experience?"

Shudder. The last thing Sabrina would do was *purposely* put herself in the spotlight. That was her family's thing. Her mom was a famous erotic painter, her vagabond dad was a photographer who sold celebrity pictures to the highest bidder, and her half brother was a nude street performer wearing body paint to resemble popular science fiction characters. She'd felt like an outsider in her own family. Her childhood had been a circus of brilliance and showmanship and drama, and she'd gotten out as soon as she could. Was it any wonder she hated being the center of attention? Her friends had no clue about that, and she wasn't about to share.

Cherry on top? Her family didn't believe in committed relationships. Her parents had never married. Her entire family going back generations had relationships all over the place, rarely married, or if they did, separated or divorced quickly. There were kids everywhere with all different parents, everyone walking to the beat of a different drummer. She was sure media attention on her would bring her family out of the woodwork. They lived for this stuff. Meanwhile, she'd be losing clients left and right as they lost faith in her supposed expertise. No relationship and a lifetime of bad examples did not inspire confidence. Add in the fact that her one and only committed relationship had left her at the altar and it was strike three. *Fraud, fraud, fraud.*

Heat crept up her neck as her friends stared at her expectantly. "I'm definitely not a PR person. I really don't like the spotlight."

"Fact number three," Lexi declared, raising three fingers in the air, "if you go on this talk show, you'll be able to help so many people. They *need* to hear from you."

Sabrina swallowed hard. That was the heart of it. Could she get past her own misgivings for the greater good? She had helped a lot of couples in her private practice.

Mad, a tough no-filter woman, leaned forward, elbows on her knees. Her dyed fire-engine red hair fell into her eyes, and she shoved it away. "If you didn't want the spotlight, why'd you write the article in the first place?"

Sabrina squirmed. The real reason was so humiliating. "I don't know."

Mad jabbed a finger at Sabrina. "You've got the worst lying face I've ever seen. You're blushing like crazy."

Hailey piped up. "Sabrina's always been a blusher." She leaned down to her giant pink doggie purse, her long strawberry blond hair obscuring the view. A moment later, she tossed her hair back and her little dog Rose appeared, drawing a collective "awww" from the women. Rose's wiry white fur was made up in a tiny ponytail on top of her head with a red bow that matched her red doggie sweater. Since getting Rose two days ago, Hailey had bought a wardrobe of coordinating doggie sweaters and bows. Rose quickly settled into Hailey's lap.

"What's the real reason, huh?" Mad pressed, giving Sabrina a knowing look. "That article ripped commitment-phobes to shreds. Who pissed you off?"

Everyone looked at Sabrina curiously. Mad smirked.

"Okay! I admit it!" Sabrina exclaimed. "It was a revenge piece. I got a wedding invitation from the jerk who left me at the altar." What a slap in the face! As if living through his betrayal wasn't enough. As if her lack of committed relationships ever since wasn't enough. As if she *wanted* to watch the bastard have the kind of happiness that rightfully should've been hers.

Everyone stared at her in shock. She was normally not prone to outbursts.

She clenched her teeth, irritated that she'd lost her cool. "I know it was unprofessional."

She'd chosen her career out of her own morbid need to know what made relationships work after her so-certain relationship fell apart. For a long time she hadn't known why Kevin had left her at the altar. There was no other woman. He came from a stable, loving family. In retrospect, his family was a major part of his appeal. His parents and sister were so *normal,* and she'd longed to be part of that family. Two years later, his sister had gotten in touch and shared that Kevin had been adrift since their almost wedding, single and job-hopping. Obviously Sabrina had chosen wrong, but Kevin's impulsive risk-taking streak hadn't been clear as a college student. Watching him flee the church had been a devastating shock. And now he was getting married. Probably an impulse decision with someone completely unsuitable, she thought uncharitably.

Mad shook her head, smiling. "Girl! I didn't think you had it in you. That's fucking awesome!" She walked over and fist-bumped Sabrina.

"Thank you," Sabrina said, not entirely sure Mad's approval was warranted. As a relationship counselor, she should be above pettiness. It was something she always emphasized to her clients: rise above, think of the big picture. Despite Sabrina's momentary lapse—big-picture view—she had the quiet life she'd always dreamed of as a kid. Until now. *See what happens when you lose your cool?*

Hailey stroked Rose behind the ear, and the dog closed her eyes, letting out a contented sigh. "Sabrina, your ex was a complete screwup and totally missed out on you."

The women murmured agreement, making Sabrina feel a little better.

Hailey went on. "But now that the article's out there, your popularity is growing by the hour. Definitely take advantage of that. Your career could explode!"

The hair on the back of Sabrina's neck stood up at the thought of that kind of exposure and the potential damage to her professional reputation. Her practice that she'd built from nothing over the last three years would tank if her clients lost faith in her.

Lexi, sitting by her side, grabbed her hand and spoke earnestly. "If you don't do this talk-show interview, you'll regret it for the rest of your life. You'll always wonder, how many people could I have reached that needed to hear from me at that exact moment? There's a lot of lonely people in the world."

Sabrina studied Lexi for a moment. Was Lexi the lonely one?

"It's okay to be nervous," Lexi said. "Just don't let it hold you back."

Sabrina nodded once. The advice was sound, even if it was easier said than done. Not to mention she was several degrees past nervous into serious fear territory.

Hailey spoke in a soothing tone. She'd mellowed considerably since getting her doggie companion. "Sweetie, if all you need is a little confidence boost so you don't feel like a fraud, why not bring a backup guy to the interview? All he has to do is stand in the background. When they ask about your personal relationship, and they will, you can say you're engaged. If they ask anything further, just say your relationship is private. They'd expect a counselor to say something like that. Then when all the buzz dies down, just pretend you broke up, and go back to your life."

"I'm a terrible liar," Sabrina said.

"Didn't I say that?" Mad barked.

Hailey shot Mad a quelling look before turning back to Sabrina. "It's a romantic white lie for the greater good. Go into that interview confident in your relationship-expert status."

Sabrina blushed furiously, muttering, "Not an expert."

Everyone encouraged Sabrina to go for it.

"Once in a lifetime!"

"Grab this opportunity!"

"Don't be a wuss!" That last one was Mad.

Sabrina held up a palm. "Even if I had a committed relationship, this talk-show gig is just not me. I feel like I'd be faking it, like an actress. I'm not flashy. I prefer helping people one-on-one."

"Ooh!" Hailey said, her pale blue eyes bright. "Call Claire for some tips. She can coach you through it." Claire Jordan was their movie-star friend, well used to the spotlight.

"I'm not a show pony," Sabrina said stubbornly. "I just want to help people."

Lexi lifted a lock of Sabrina's hair. "With this mane of luxurious hair? Definite show-pony material."

Everyone laughed. Sabrina gave Lexi a small smile. "Ha-ha."

Haley went on enthusiastically. "You'll be faking your way through anyway, pretending not to be nervous. Add in the fake relationship, no big thing."

"Fake it 'til you make it," Lexi put in. "Make that your mantra."

Sabrina let out a breath of exasperation. "Who in the world would I even ask to be my fake fiancé?"

Lexi grinned evilly. "How about your *friend* Logan?"

Sabrina felt herself flush, her stomach dipping just hearing his name. Her secret lust for Logan Campbell was so embarrassing because it was completely one-sided. He was her breathtaking, spine-tingling, panty-melting sexy *friend*, ever since he'd rented the office upstairs from hers six months ago. He joked around with her all the time but never, ever flirted. She knew all the classic male flirtation signals—a deepening of voice, direct sustained eye contact, throwing his shoulders back to appear bigger—and he did exactly zero. His voice was always deep and never changed. She wasn't sure how long he'd hold her eye contact because she looked away the moment she felt her cheeks heat, but when she looked back, he was always looking somewhere just past her ear. His shoulders were always the same, wide and muscularly athletic like all of the Campbell men, but never thrown back, always just relaxed.

Even if Logan did think of her in *that way,* which he didn't, he was still not for her. If there was one thing she'd learned as a relationship counselor, it was spotting the men who were not good for her relationship-wise. Logan was a classic commitment-phobe.

She smoothed her hair. "I told you we're just friends."

Mad cocked her head. "Yeah, ask Logan. It'll be nothing for him." Logan was her older brother. "He's been hung up on his college girlfriend for years."

Sabrina stared at Mad in shock. Logan had never once mentioned this college girlfriend, and they had lunch on a weekly basis, when neither of them was too busy. Dedicated to the same woman for years? Had she misjudged him? Maybe she should've given him a lusty signal. Not that it mattered. He wasn't into her, and now that she knew he had ex-girlfriend baggage, forget it.

Hailey offered an alternative with Mad's other single brother. "Josh'll do it if you pay him." She scowled. "Just expect to pay big." Hailey knew this from personal experience. She was a wedding planner and, in desperate need of a dependable wedding date, had paid Josh to escort her to weddings so she wouldn't always be alone in front of clients. Unfortunately, their deal had quickly soured, and they'd been fighting ever since.

Sabrina huffed. She wasn't a charity case, for crying out loud! She didn't need to beg her friend to be her fake fiancé or, God forbid, *pay* someone. She was a professional. "I'll do the interview on my own," she declared and immediately felt light-headed. *Fraud, fraud, fraud* echoed in her head, gradually fading to a loud ringing in her ears.

Next thing she knew, someone pushed her head down between her knees.

"Breathe," Lexi ordered.

"I'm texting Logan," Mad said.

"No," Sabrina croaked.

"Maybe I'll go as your fiancée," Lexi said, making Sabrina laugh a little. Lexi might be terribly jaded about men, but she had a real appreciation for their form, the bigger and more muscled, the better.

Sabrina straightened. "I'm okay. Let's go get a drink." They always went to Garner's Sports Bar & Grill after book club for drinks.

The women all gave her sympathetic looks.

"What?" she asked.

"We haven't even started our meeting, silly," Hailey said, pulling her e-reader from her white leather purse. "And I know just what we should read." She bit back a smile, her pale blue eyes lit with amusement. "*Married to my Fake Fiancé.*"

Everyone laughed. Sabrina groaned.

2

—————

The next morning, Sabrina returned to work and scheduled the talk show for Monday morning. Her voice shook, but she did it. Then she left a message for her friend Claire to call her for a coaching session on how to do a TV interview. She could *so* do this.

She rescheduled her Monday morning appointments and reviewed her calendar. She'd booked a week off at the end of the month and was now extra glad she had. Her January break was very necessary after the rush of holiday appointments. Tensions ran high over the holidays, and she saw her clients in full rotation between Christmas and New Year, when more people were home and fighting. She planned to do nothing but putter around her apartment, trying out new recipes and binge-watching her favorite TV shows. Heaven!

She made it through her morning appointments relatively put together, considering she was three days away from a huge TV interview and she still hadn't heard back from Claire. Of course, Claire was on California time, so she shouldn't get too worked up yet. Her phone rang. Claire! She grabbed her phone off her desk and then realized it was her office phone. "Hello, Sabrina Clarke speaking."

"This is Tara Brinkman. Are you the author of 'Goodbye Commitment-Phobe'?"

"Yes, I am. How can I help you today?"

The woman spoke with sharp bite. "You can help me by taking down your article immediately. My book, a *New York Times* bestseller, was also titled *Goodbye Commitment-Phobe* well before yours. I'm the one known as the Commitment Counselor—that's a registered trademark, by the way—and I'd better not hear you're using the same moniker."

She shut her gaping mouth with a snap. "I'm not using that. I've never heard of you."

"I can't believe this was coincidental. You're trying to represent yourself as me, riding on the coattails of my stellar reputation."

Sabrina shoved a hand in her hair, flummoxed by the woman's hostility. "I had no idea you wrote something with a similar name."

"Not similar, the exact same. It's called copyright infringement. Take it down, or I will send my lawyer after you."

She broke out in a cold sweat. Holy crap! "I'm sure this is all just a misunderstanding. There's no need for lawyers."

"Right. I looked you up. You're in my area. I have an office in Manhattan and Fieldridge, Connecticut. You're trying to poach my clients."

She shook her head in vehement denial. "I swear this is the first I've heard of you. When did your book come out?"

"I'll be keeping a close eye on you," Tara said ominously before hanging up.

Sabrina sat there for a minute in shock. Then she opened her laptop and looked up Tara Brinkman. It was legit. All of it —her practice, her book, her local office only a couple of towns away. Shit. Her book had come out five years ago when Sabrina was still in college. *Goodbye Commitment-Phobe* wouldn't have been a book she sought out. At the time she'd been in a happily committed relationship.

She closed the laptop with trembling hands. This woman could do serious damage to Sabrina's reputation. Sabrina didn't have a lawyer either. She had no idea what to do. She wasn't even sure if it was possible to take the article down now that it had been shared all over the internet.

Her office phone rang again, and she jumped, heart pounding, staring at it like it was a cobra about to strike. *Calm down. It's probably a client.* She grabbed the phone. "Hello?"

"Sabrina Clarke?" an authoritative woman's voice asked, scaring the crap out of her. Maybe it was a lawyer about to slap her with a lawsuit.

She hesitated before finally saying, "Yes, how can I help you?"

"This is Joyce Earley. I'm a literary agent, and I'd like to talk about you writing a book. I absolutely loved 'Goodbye Commitment-Phobe, Hello Happiness!'"

She was so relieved it wasn't a lawyer, she immediately confided in this complete stranger. "I was thinking of taking the article down. I just got a call from the author of a best-selling book with the same title. There might be an issue with copyright infringement."

"Can't copyright a title. Anyway, this thing's got legs. Picture this, white cover with a bold red heart and the title in pink 'Romance Rebel.' Something that—"

"I'm not a rebel," she said firmly, surprising herself with her clear thoughts given she was so shaken up by her morning. But she'd always been clear on her boundaries. She didn't want the rebel label. She'd worked hard to be much more traditional than that, her own twisted rebellion against her crazy family. Sometimes she feared her wayward genes would keep her single forever. No wonder her friends had suggested she get a fake fiancé. They probably saw right through her to her family's uncommitted roots.

Joyce went on in a cheery tone. "Doesn't have to be that title. How about 'A Guide to Lasting Love'? Nah, something catchier. We'll work on that. You really touched a nerve with your article, and I think you could help millions of women around the world."

Sabrina rested her head in her hand and stared blankly at her desk, trying to think it through. "I would like to reach more women." So far she'd been focused mostly on couples, but she could branch out to individual therapy that helped single women work toward a fulfilling relationship by working on themselves. It would be similar to the sologamy concept—marrying yourself as a commitment to self. At least she'd done that much commitment in her life; doing a sologamy ceremony with her friends as witnesses had been awesome.

"Excellent!" Joyce exclaimed. "But we've got to strike while the iron's hot! Why don't you work up a bare-bones outline, we'll tack your article on the front, and I'll shop it. I'm sure we'll go to auction for the big bucks. Of course, we'll do a book tour, interviews, TV spots, the works. Actually, I can get you on some news shows now, which'll only make your book that much more appealing to publishers."

Fraud, fraud, fraud.

She broke out in a hot sweat this time, a little light-headed. *Do not pass out.* "Hold on." She pulled her cardigan off and rapidly fanned her blouse against her body.

She could hear Joyce calling her, saying loudly, "Are you still there?"

She grabbed the phone. "Yes. Actually, I already have a talk show booked. I'll be going on *Sunshine America* Monday morning."

"Fantastic! I can parlay that into more national interviews. The other talk shows will be dying to have you on!"

Her grip on the phone tightened. "That sounds like a lot of spotlight."

"First things first, Sabrina, would you like to write a book that helps millions of women all over the world?"

"Yes." There could be only one answer to that question. She'd dedicated her life to helping others.

"Great! I'll email you the agency contract. Look forward to working with you!"

Joyce disconnected.

Sabrina slowly lowered her head to the desk, resting her forehead on the cool surface, trying to find her calm stable center again. Things were out of control—snowballing, crazy, circus-level drama. She remained in that position for a very long time, so overwhelmed her brain stopped cranking out *fraud* and shifted to a dull white noise.

Someone knocked on her door, and she jerked upright, smoothing her hair. Shit. How long had she been quietly freaking out? Did she miss lunch? Was it time for her afternoon appointment already?

"Come in," she called.

The door opened, and Logan poked his head in. His short light brown hair and neatly trimmed beard highlighted a striking, perfectly symmetric face with warm brown eyes, a narrow nose that tilted up slightly at the end, and a killer smile. He was, by far, the best looking of the Campbell men, and they were a handsome lot. She'd heard he took after his beauty-queen mom, the masculine version of perfect fine features. He should be the one on TV.

"You free for lunch?" he asked.

She checked the time on her phone. She still had forty-five minutes. "Sure," she managed, coming back to herself after her brief meltdown.

"Great." He stepped inside, carrying a bag from the Chinese place and setting it on the coffee table between the beige client sofa and her matching beige counselor chair. He was tall, six feet, wiry with muscle like an athlete, but also really smart. He was the tech guy in his company. Checkin was an online service that did background checks on temporary caregivers and employees.

She remained at her desk, waiting to be sure she was steady enough to join him. This had been a hell of a day already, and it was only lunchtime. He took a seat on the sofa, casual and relaxed as always in a long-sleeved black cotton shirt, close-fitting faded jeans, and sneakers.

He lifted his head. "I got chicken and broccoli and pork lo mein, figured we could share." He flashed a smile that lit up his gorgeous face, and she felt herself flush. Even from a distance the effect was spectacular. "Got your favorite fried dumplings too." He set out paper plates, napkins, and plastic forks he'd brought from his own office's kitchen.

"Thanks, Logan. This is just what I needed." She closed the distance, pleased that her legs were steady, and took the chair across from him. She crossed her legs in her charcoal gray pencil skirt and grabbed one of the bottled waters he'd brought, twisting the cap off.

She was always careful to keep a table between them. Not like she was going to throw herself at him, it just seemed easier to keep the friendship boundaries clear. It baffled her why she lusted for him so badly, even knowing how unsuitable he was for her. There was the commitment-phobe thing, though now she wasn't so sure if he actually was that, given the recent shocking news that he still pined for his ex.

Either way—commitment-phobe or ex baggage—Logan was a bad bet. On top of that, he was a risk-taker. Sabrina had worked hard for a stable no-risk lifestyle. Just look at how he'd quit a lucrative job at his brother's company to strike out on his own with Checkin. He'd slept on his friend's couch for a year, barely scraping by. Okay, yes, her tolerance for risk was extremely low compared to other people, she knew that about herself, knew she needed security and stability more than the average person because of her previous relationship and her unconventional childhood, but there it was. That chance-taking streak within Logan, which might've been just fine for someone else, was simply too much of a risk for *her*.

She let out a quiet sigh. She just needed to find a risk-averse, relationship-ready man to let loose her pent-up lust.

She stared at his large masculine hands as he set the food out. Logan always remembered her favorite dishes from local restaurants. He was a very thoughtful friend, unusual in a man in her experience. Still, just a friend. They took turns paying for lunch, so it wasn't like this was a date. She tore her gaze away from his hands and—since he was focused on the food—looked her fill at his handsome face instead. Not for the first time she wondered what his beard would feel like. Soft the way his hair looked, or rough like stubble?

She took a long drink of cooling water, wishing she could get over this embarrassing lust for her friend.

His brown eyes twinkled with amusement. "Mad tells me you want me to be your fake fiancé."

She spewed water, her cheeks burning. When she could finally speak, she told him, "Your sister has a big mouth."

He chuckled low and deep. "Yup. I told her it was ridiculous."

She wiped her mouth dry with a napkin. Did he mean the two of them together were ridiculous or the concept of a fake fiancé was ridiculous? "Why exactly is it ridiculous?"

He lifted one finely formed shoulder. "All the work of pretending, none of the fun."

Her stomach dipped. What fun did he mean exactly? Was this not as one-sided as she'd thought? She blustered on. "That was Hailey's idea, and it's messed up."

He inclined his head and dug out some chicken and broccoli, put them on his plate, and pushed the container across the table to her. "Mad says you've got a big opportunity as a relationship expert. She sent me the link to your article. Some fierce stuff in there."

She wasn't sure if fierce stuff was good or bad, but just hearing "relationship expert" made her adrenaline spike—heart racing, breath short, sweat forming on her upper lip. *Fraud, fraud, fraud.* TV, cameras, lights, millions of people watching her say what? She had no idea what she was going to say, had no idea what they were going to ask. What if she blurted she'd become a relationship counselor because she'd been left at the altar? What if they looked into her noncommitted background? It would ruin her reputation, destroy her practice. *Fraud, fraud, fraud.*

What if that psycho commitment counselor started giving interviews calling Sabrina out? What if she got tangled up in a lawsuit? AHHH!!!

Logan waved a hand near her face. "You okay? You're paler than usual."

She blinked, refocusing on him, the insult hiding in his casual remark bringing her back to reality. *Paler than usual?* See? Complete lack of interest. Someone who was interested in her wouldn't say paler than usual, they'd say something nicer, like "a little pale." Logan didn't care about niceties like that. He saw her like a buddy.

Which was *fine.*

She had standards. So what if that meant she hadn't found

anyone to get serious about since her stupid trip down the aisle.

"Sabrina?"

"What?"

"Any special reason you're acting weird? I mean, besides the interview."

"I'm not acting weird." She piled some of each dish on her plate and stared at it, her appetite deserting her. She met his eyes. "I'm going on *Sunshine America* Monday morning. Live. So if I screw up—" she slashed a hand through the air "—that's it."

He raised a brow. "You're not gonna screw up. You're an expert. They're just going to ask you stuff that you already know."

She threw her hands up. "Why does everyone keep calling me an expert? I'm not an expert at all!"

He took a bite of broccoli and eyed her. Finally, he said, "*The Clover Park Record* called you a relationship healer."

She waved that away. "That's not the same thing. Besides, it's just a local paper."

"You have a lot of happy clients."

"They want to do the work of a relationship. I just help them along." Her shoulders drooped, and she stared at her untouched lunch. "I'm not an expert."

"Okay, you're not an expert."

Her head jerked up. "But they think I am! I'm a complete fraud."

His fork stopped in midair. "How exactly are you a fraud?"

"Because I'm giving all this advice on how to have a committed relationship when I don't even have one."

He stared at her. "Have you ever had one? That should count."

"Yes, but it was a while ago." She waved her hands wildly. "And then this psycho relationship counselor—"

"You mean there's two psycho relationship counselors?" He grinned. "I thought you cornered the market."

She threw a napkin at him. He laughed and handed it back.

She leaned forward across the table, lowering her voice. "This woman called and accused me of trying to steal her clients by copying her famous book title that I didn't even know about. She threatened me with a lawsuit."

His brown eyes widened. "Seriously?"

She leaned back. "Yes! She was extremely hostile. But then a literary agent called and said you can't copyright titles. I still think I have to watch my back where that counselor is concerned. And, in other shocking news, that literary agent wants me to write a book."

His eyes lit up with his smile. "Sabrina, that's great!"

She found herself smiling. "Thanks, I'm actually really happy about that part." Sharing all this stuff with Logan made her relax enough to start eating. She speared a dumpling. "She wants to call it *Romance Rebel*."

He barked out a laugh. "That doesn't sound like you."

She chewed and swallowed. "No kidding. And she wants to do this whole book tour and publicity thing with interviews and TV spots, and..." She took a deep breath. "Omigod, that is so not me."

He studied her for a moment. "Because you're shy?"

She narrowed her eyes. "I'm not shy."

His lips curled up in a small smile. "Yeah, you are."

"I'm perfectly fine one-on-one, I just don't like the spotlight."

He twirled his fork in the lo mein. "Because you're shy."

"I'm not shy! I'm just an indiscriminate blusher!"

"Such a shy blusher," he teased. "I'm watching you, Wazowski," he added in his impersonation of Roz from the movie *Monsters, Inc.*

A reluctant smile tugged at her lips. He did do funny impressions. "You don't listen."

"I listen. I just don't agree." He winked and went back to his lunch.

She glared at him, irritated that he just didn't get that it wasn't shyness holding her back, but he was too busy eating lunch to notice. "I don't want to be doing all this stuff with the media. That's not compatible with my life in any way, shape, or form."

He tipped his bottled water up to his lips and spoke around it. "Why not?"

"Because my entire life was chaos, and I can't even believe I'm telling you this. Let's just say I emerged from the chaos and created my own stability."

He tilted his head. "Are you telling me your family is nuts?"

"Yes."

"So's mine. So's everyone's."

"No, yours is loud and happy." She knew and loved his family—his sister, Mad, his older brothers, and his dad, a total sweetheart. Of course, they weren't perfect. His mom had left the family when he was only four and never called or visited during his entire childhood. That could really shake a person's belief in lasting relationships, which had made his commitment phobia understandable. Though now that she knew he was pining for a lost love, she wasn't sure her diagnosis was correct. She knew a lot more about him than he probably realized through her friendship with Mad.

He stabbed some chicken. "Not always happy."

"Mine is embarrassing, flashy—"

"Flashy?"

"Nobody ever stays married, no lasting commitments of any kind. Kids everywhere like they've never heard of birth control. Drama, drama, drama. And they love it! I barely escaped with my sanity."

He shook his head. "I can't picture you in that family."

"Exactly. Not fun."

They ate in comfortable silence for a few minutes.

She set her fork down. "I want to help people. I just don't want to lose myself in the chaos."

Logan lifted his head. "Who's going with you to your TV interview?"

She took a drink, thinking it over. Her friends were probably all working. "I don't know. I'll ask my friends tomorrow when we're shopping for Mad's wedding dress, but I'm not hopeful. The interview's at eight a.m. on Monday morning in the city. I have to be there by six. Claire would be my ideal choice, but she's still out of town."

He met her eyes, his expression unusually serious. "You want me there, say the word."

Her heart squeezed, touched by the offer. She knew he was busy at work with some important investor meetings he had to prepare for. A small sliver of hope warmed her despite her certainty that he saw her only as a friend, despite all of her previous concerns about getting close to him.

"Why would you want to do that?" she asked softly.

"Because we're friends and you're shy as hell." One corner of his mouth lifted. "You know they have a studio audience *and* people on the street can watch through the big windows. I've passed by their studio before. I'd hate to see you blushing brighter than their logo." The *Sunshine America* logo was bright red and orange. *Gee, thanks.*

She lifted her chin. "I'm a professional. I can handle myself."

He took a drink, watching her over the rim. "You sure?"

"Yes!"

"Okay, okay." His brown eyes held a hint of amusement. "Pretty mouthy for a shy girl."

Grr…

He grinned. "Though your article was badass."

She met his eyes and smiled. He smiled back so warmly that her entire body warmed. Maybe there was something there. Questions darted through her mind: you into me? You into committed relationships? Are you really still pining for your college girlfriend? Would you be willing to embrace a stable, no-risk lifestyle?

So like a total professional, she blurted, "With so many of our friends getting married, you ever think about it for yourself?"

He blew out a breath. "That was random."

Her cheeks and neck were burning, but she still managed

to say in a composed voice, "I'm a relationship counselor. It's my special field of interest."

He shook his head. "Most things don't pan out, in my experience. Hard to imagine committing to forever when the odds of sticking together are stacked against you." His lips quirked to the side in a wry expression. "Guess that's why the world needs people like you to help them stick. No offense to your profession, but it seems to me if it's that difficult to be together, then maybe they shouldn't be."

She suppressed a sigh of disappointment. How unromantic, how commitment-phobic, how honest. She did have to give him credit for being honest. And she had the answer she needed. Logan wasn't a good fit for her relationship-wise. A committed relationship was something you had to work for. It was a choice, every day, to commit to the love of your life, even when that was difficult. It occurred to her he hadn't mentioned his ex in all this relationship talk. Mad must've been way off base on that. He was definitely not pining.

Logan launched into a detailed rundown of his upcoming investor meetings out in California and what it could mean for Checkin. He'd built the business, valued at two hundred fifty million, with his honorary brother Ben, and now they were seeking investment to take it higher. The most important meeting was in two weeks.

She listened intently without interruption as he spoke passionately about the business and what he dreamed for it. At least they had this, a close friendship, where they could talk about important stuff. That had to be enough.

3

Logan drove to Manhattan early Monday morning to surprise Sabrina by showing up for her big talk-show debut. If he'd told her ahead of time he'd be there, she would've put on a brave face and said she was just fine. But he'd seen the real fear in her eyes and, as soon as he found out from Mad that Sabrina was going alone, it was a no-brainer. Sabrina was like a porcelain doll—beautiful, perfect, delicate. Untouchable. Her dark blond hair was smooth and straight, never mussed or out of place, and she had these big innocent-looking brown eyes with round cheeks prone to blushing, and a sweet smile. Her body was trim and curvy, wrapped in perfectly tailored professional clothes.

Not that he was a complete Neanderthal, but he needed someone that could challenge him, a little more give-and-take. He could easily walk all over Sabrina with her sweet accommodating ways. And, for sure, if Sabrina was rattled, a talk-show host could walk all over her too. If his standing backstage during her big interview could give back even a *little* of the support she'd given him, well, it was the least he could do. His sister-in-law Claire had gotten him on the VIP list so he could stand in Sabrina's line of vision, off camera, letting her know a friend was there for her.

Sabrina didn't know how much her quiet listening and support had helped him through some tough spots. Like last summer when his business partner, Ben, had been falsely accused of sexual harassment. Logan had been hurting for his friend and worried about their company when the news leaked out through business channels. Sabrina had encouraged him to ignore the whispers and let Ben know he believed in him. They'd weathered that storm.

Then later when Ben had been a bear to work with and Logan couldn't figure out why, Sabrina was the one who'd zeroed in on the cause of Ben's misery—Missy—and suggested Logan let her go a little early from her work contract so Missy and Ben could get together without professional boundaries holding them back. Now they were engaged. Sabrina was smart like that. Too modest for her own good, but, in his opinion, she was *the* relationship expert.

Damn traffic. It had been smooth sailing all the way into the city. He inched his way through the last few blocks to the *Sunshine America* studio, hoping it cleared up fast. He was excited for Sabrina and what this could mean for her career. Sabrina's believing in him had really helped his own career. When he, the tech guy, had to take the lead on the investor meetings due to Ben's damaged rep from that lying former employee, Sabrina had offered unwavering support, listening to him go on and on about his presentation and then confirming he was on the right track. Ben liked to razz him about Sabrina, calling her Logan's sweetheart, which was part of the problem with Sabrina. She was too sweet; she even smelled sweet like honey and flowers.

Though she'd surprised him during their lunch on Friday, raising her voice for the first time ever and confessing her family was nuts. He'd always pictured her in a quiet family that went to orchestra concerts or the opera. In any case, she'd never given him any indication that she wanted to be more than friends. She was so reserved and professional. He couldn't imagine even mussing up her perfect hair. The one and only time she'd touched him had been last week on New Year's Eve when she'd given him the most awkward hug of his life. Even his most reserved brother, Josh, gave better bro hugs than that. She'd been so careful to keep her distance during their hug she'd actually squeezed his elbow—the most unexciting spot on the human body—and patted his back. When the hug ended, she'd jumped a foot away like she could barely tolerate touching him.

There were other complications. Sabrina was close with his loudmouthed sister, which was why he never got too personal during their talks. He hadn't told Sabrina about Olivia, even though things were looking very promising for him and Olivia. He'd fallen hard for her his senior year of college and proposed on graduation night. Something he'd kept from his family and friends because she'd turned him down, saying he wasn't from the right family. Translation: he had no money. She was from a wealthy family, and her inheritance depended on her marrying well, all sorts of stipulations, blah, blah, blah. All he'd heard was *you're not good enough.* He'd thrown himself into work, mostly to prove he could be a success and shove it in her face. But that was in the early days. Eventually, he'd really enjoyed work and later building his own business.

Olivia's rejection didn't sting as much as it might have because she kept in touch, sending him birthday and holiday cards, occasionally emailing to see how he was doing. Deep down he knew her keeping in touch meant she still cared for him. A couple of months ago, she'd emailed with her usual friendly note, and when he'd told her Checkin was about to take it to the next level, she'd been happy for him. She'd even said she should've known he'd be a success and she'd been foolish to turn his proposal down. Now, he wasn't naïve. He read between the lines that he was more appealing to her now as an established successful businessman than an entry-level employee from a working-class family, but still. There'd been something real between them before, and now that he was at a point in his life where he could reap the rewards of all his hard work, he'd been thinking more about making time for a relationship.

It helped that Olivia had confessed the real reason she'd

rejected him was because she'd been too young. She was two years younger than him, only twenty when he'd proposed. He forgave her. She'd been sincere, and it had been her initial rejection, after all, that lit the fire of ambition in him.

He'd flown out to San Francisco six weeks ago to see her over the long Thanksgiving weekend. They'd connected like the fit of an old glove—comfortable and easy. He hadn't seen her since—she'd flown to the Swiss Alps for Christmas with her family, and he'd wanted to spend Christmas with his own family while sneaking a little work in. But they'd talked and texted a lot. He'd told her if things went well for Checkin, he'd open a San Francisco office so they could be together. She'd been excited about the idea.

He hadn't told Olivia about Sabrina either, even though they were just friends. Olivia was the jealous type. Besides, if everything worked out like he hoped for Checkin, he'd be moving to San Francisco, and Sabrina would be out of his life. No more lunches, no more deep conversations. His throat tightened, unexpectedly choked up at the thought. He'd miss Sabrina. No one had ever listened to him the way she did. He gave himself a mental shake. Priorities. His life was on the verge of great things.

He reached the studio an excruciatingly long time later and drove past it, looking for a parking garage. He found one a couple of blocks from the studio, left the keys with the valet, and booked it out of there. Her interview was starting in fifteen minutes. He went into the studio building and stopped at the security guard's desk, giving his name and telling him he was on the list.

The security guard, a tough-looking man with a shaved head and deep lines in his face, looked skeptical. "Driver's license."

Logan pulled out his wallet and showed him. "It's starting soon. I need to get in there."

"Hold on." The guy picked up a phone and checked in about Logan. He hung up and turned to him. "Set's closed. All the seats in the audience are filled."

"No, I'm with Claire Jordan. I'm supposed to go backstage. She cleared it with the producer."

He looked around Logan, where there was no Claire Jordan. "Uh-huh." No one ever believed he knew Claire Jordan. She was just that famous, but she'd married his brother Jake.

"Claire's my sister-in-law," he said urgently. "She cleared it. Check with the producer."

The man eyed him. "What's the producer's name?"

He racked his brain. "Cindy. No, Sandy. Sally! She said Sally would help me out."

The man's gaze flicked over his shoulder, where another person was approaching the desk. Shit. This guy wasn't moving fast enough, and Logan was going to miss the whole thing. He pulled out his phone and called Claire. She was going to kill him. It was before five a.m. in California. Voicemail. She must've turned her phone off. He called Jake. Voicemail.

The security guard let the other guy in.

Logan gestured to the security phone. "Please call again. Claire got me on the list."

"Buddy, you're not on any list."

"I am!" His gaze darted to the elevator. He debated racing past the guy, but the chances of getting to Sabrina before he was hauled out of the building were slim. He focused on the security guard again. "Check with Sally."

"There is no Sally."

"Cindy, then."

The man stood, bulky with muscle and fully armed. "Sir, I'm going to have to ask you to leave."

Logan scrambled for an alternative. He had to let Sabrina know she wasn't facing this alone. He lifted a hand, signaling the guy to stand down, turned, and left the building, still trying to think of a workaround.

A crowd was gathered at the end of the street near the large picture windows of the studio. All right then, that was how it was going to have to be.

～

Sabrina sat stiffly in the pale yellow cushioned guest chair near the ultra-perky hosts, Becky Simpson and Dell Rowan, sitting in matching chairs. The makeup lady blotted Sabrina's face with some powder for the second time. No one ever died of stage fright, she reassured herself. The worst that could happen was she'd blurt out every single reason she was a fraud and run out of the place. Live on TV. Gah! *No negative self-talk. Be your own cheerleader.*

"Try not to sweat so much," the makeup lady said before heading over to Becky and Dell.

Sabrina took in a shaky breath, clasping her hands tightly in her lap. The studio audience was filled and noisily excited to be here. A huge crowd outside waved and pointed, peering inside the large picture windows at them. Some people held signs that read I love Dell! There were a lot of signs that read Good Morning, Sunshine! That was the line they used to start every show.

Claire had prepped her last night by phone, but truthfully, it had made Sabrina even more nervous than before. Claire was adamant that Sabrina only answer questions she wanted to, but her suggested "no comment" wasn't something Sabrina felt comfortable saying. A movie star could get away with that, but a relationship counselor had to come across as warm and open. She wished she were a better actress because then she could play the part she longed to be seen as—a confident, warm, open relationship counselor with a committed relationship and a normal family, who'd never been a jilted bride.

"Five minutes!" someone hollered offstage.

Sabrina gulped.

Becky and Dell hadn't said anything beyond "good morning" to her and had been busy chatting with the crew and each other. Sabrina supposed she was just another guest to them, but she sure wished there were someone for her to chat with so she could get out of her own head and relax a little.

A woman walked over and checked Sabrina's microphone clipped to her white cardigan. She wore her favorite purple A-line dress and black heels. She'd put the entire outfit on last night and texted a picture to Claire, who'd approved it both for its professionalism and pop of color. At least she knew she had that going for her.

A young woman wearing a headset put a *Sunshine America* mug filled with water on the end table next to Sabrina's chair.

"Thank you," Sabrina croaked. "I'm parched."

The young woman took pity on her, leaned close, and whispered, "Most guests use the water when they need a moment before answering a question."

"Smart. Thanks."

"Good luck!"

Sabrina smiled tightly and took a small sip of water. Then she was alone again under the hot lights. A few minutes later, the audience quieted as the screen flashed the countdown to filming. Sabrina tucked her icy fingers under her legs.

Becky and Dell finally stopped talking to each other and gave her a warm smile.

She smiled back, her cheeks hurting with the false effort. *Be genuine, be yourself.* She took a slow deep breath.

The director did a silent countdown, the cameras aimed at them. She'd been instructed not to look at the camera, just to look at Becky and Dell. It was hard not to notice the three huge cameras aimed in their direction.

"Good morning, sunshine!" Becky exclaimed, looking into the camera.

"Good morning to all of our viewers," Dell chimed in smoothly in his rich baritone voice. "We have a very special guest today. If you've made a New Year's resolution to find the love of your life, Sabrina Clarke might just be the answer."

"Hi, Sabrina! Welcome!" Becky said with a huge smile.

"Hi, Becky and Dell. I'm happy to be here." Her voice shook. Dammit.

"We loved your piece 'Goodbye Commitment-Phobe,

Hello Happiness!'" Becky looked off camera toward the crew. "Can we get a link up there? In case anyone missed it."

A moment later, Becky smiled. "There it is! Thank you. Sabrina, what motivated you to write it? Was it personal experience or based on your clients?"

Sabrina's heart pounded in her ears. If she said it was personal experience, there would be follow-up questions, and she did *not* want to share that on national television. If she said it was her clients, then that was a clear breach of patient confidentiality. And she was definitely not going to mention the real vengeful reason. "I don't know" wasn't going to cut it here.

"Neither," she blurted.

"What was the impetus behind it?" Becky asked. "Had you recently found some happiness you were eager to share?"

Sabrina blinked, her mind blanking. This was a show about good news. She had to say something positive. Her eye caught on a sign someone was holding up outside the window. It read Shy Girl Rocks! She couldn't help her huge smile. Only Logan would tease her like that. He was here. He knew what this meant to her, knew how nervous she was and, even though she told him she could handle it, he'd showed up to support her. He cared about her deeply. Her chest swelled with affection. If only she could see him. He was near the back of the crowd.

Becky turned toward the window and back to Sabrina. "Is there someone you know outside?"

Sabrina smiled. "Sorry, yes. What were you saying?"

Dell chimed in with a teasing tone. "Someone special? Does he have a name?"

Sabrina's cheeks burned. "Logan."

Becky slapped her leg. "Well, let's get Logan in here. Stay tuned. Right after the commercial break."

Sabrina relaxed a little. It would really help if she knew Logan was in the audience cheering her on. She'd answer Becky and Dell's questions just like she was having a casual lunch chat with Logan. He was always so relaxed and laid-back.

The young woman who'd brought Sabrina's water stopped by. "What's his full name, and what does he look like?"

"Logan Campbell. He's six feet, probably wearing a black down jacket, short light brown hair and beard." *The sexy one.*

"Got it."

Sabrina glanced over at Becky and Dell, who were in deep conversation. At least with Logan here, she knew someone was on her side. They'd probably laugh about this later.

Minutes ticked by during the commercial break, and she realized she'd never answered Becky's question. She'd say she was inspired to write her article because she'd seen some of her friends struggle and wanted to help people like them. It was technically true because some of her friends had been through doozies of ex-boyfriends, and she could technically count herself as a friend too. Pleased with her answer, she looked forward to continuing with the interview.

She turned as if with a sixth sense, her gaze colliding with Logan's. He lifted a hand in a small hello, standing just off camera. She jumped up and rushed over to him. His familiar features in this strange place so dear to her she impulsively hugged him, breathing in his fresh clean scent.

She pulled away, beaming. "I can't believe you're here!"

He grinned, his warm brown eyes crinkling at the corners. "Surprise. Claire was supposed to get me on the list, but there was some kind of mix-up, and I couldn't get in."

"Well, you're here now. I really appreciate it." She lowered her voice. "No one will even talk to me here."

He glanced over her shoulder at the hosts. "They'll talk to you as soon as the camera's on. You have an answer prepared? I watched the live feed on my phone, and it looked like you froze up."

"I got it now. I just needed a moment to think. It's hard to spout stuff off the cuff."

He gave her arm a squeeze, warming her at the spot. "You got this."

She wanted to hug him again, but a crew member called her back on set. She slowly backed away, gazing at Logan with equal parts gratitude and warm gooey affection. He smiled encouragingly at her. She whirled and went back to the set, fully prepared to rock this interview.

"Welcome back!" Becky chirped the moment they went back on air. "We brought Logan Campbell into the studio, and our guest is all smiles now. Guess we know the happiness that led to Sabrina's inspirational article."

Sabrina's cheeks heated, and she glanced over at Logan. His black down jacket was off, and a crew member was trying to attach a microphone to Logan's shirt while Logan backed away.

"Let's get Logan out here," Dell said. "Ladies, you'd like him to join us, wouldn't you?"

The audience clapped and hollered for Logan.

Logan raised a hand, shaking his head. Good. He was standing his ground. He gestured to her, like she was the star.

A surge of affection made her want to hug him again. He was willing to be supportive in the background, careful to respect her boundaries. This was her big moment, even if it was hard for her to claim it, and he respected that.

"Aren't they cute?" Becky asked. "How long have you been together?"

"Six months," Sabrina replied and then realized how that sounded. They'd been friends for six months. "I mean…" She looked to Logan, who was frozen like a statue, his expression blank.

"Looks serious," Dell put in.

"I appreciate what we have," Sabrina said. Okay, so it sounded like Logan was her boyfriend. At least she hadn't said fiancé. She blamed her friends for putting the idea into her subconscious. Damn. She hoped Becky and Dell didn't ask any more questions about Logan.

Becky smiled brightly at her. "How important is sexual compatibility in a relationship?"

"Top of my list," Sabrina blurted and promptly blushed the mother of all blushes from head to toe. She didn't dare look at Logan. He was probably smirking and would tease her mercilessly later.

"Sounds like you enjoy being on top," Becky said in a suggestive voice. "Ladies, we like taking responsibility for our own happiness—" she made a big exaggerated wink "—don't we?"

Her mind flashed to Logan, naked, under her. Riding him with wild abandon, his hands on her—

She grabbed her mug and took a healthy swallow of cool water. The audience applauded loudly, enthusiastic about being on top. It was mostly women here.

Dell smiled good-naturedly. "I learn so much on this show."

Everyone laughed.

Dell went on. "Sabrina, if you could give just one piece of advice to someone looking for love, what would it be?"

Sabrina relaxed. Thank God they were off the sex stuff. "Love yourself first. When you're secure in who you are and what you want in life, it makes it easy to let go of toxic relationships and welcome in love."

"That is beautiful," Becky said. She turned to the audience. "Isn't that beautiful?"

The audience applauded.

Dell chimed in with a question. "When a client comes to you with commitment issues, what's the first thing you ask?"

Now she was back on familiar territory. She answered all the rest of their questions with professional confidence.

Once the interview was over, she practically floated over to Logan. She'd made it through her first time on TV, and now she could share the whole experience with him. Hopefully he wouldn't tease her too much.

She stopped in front of him. "I think it went well."

"Yup." He jerked his chin. "Come on, they said there's a back exit to avoid the crowd by the windows."

She followed him out to a narrow hallway. "You want to ride back with me? Claire got me a car service. It's a Mercedes with tinted windows."

"I have my car," he said tersely.

She studied him, his jaw set tight. "Everything okay?"

"No."

They passed a couple of crew members talking and laughing.

"We'll talk outside," Logan said.

She bit her lower lip. He must be mad that she'd implied he was her boyfriend. Obviously he felt used. He probably respected her less for lying too. She felt awful. She knew the importance of boundaries, and she'd crossed one big time.

They reached the sidewalk outside, near the end of the block and a safe distance from the crowd by the windows.

She touched his jacket sleeve lightly. "Logan, I'm really sorry. I shouldn't have implied you were my boyfriend. It just kinda came out."

He scrubbed a hand over his face. "I have a girlfriend. She's not going to be happy to hear this on TV. She's the jealous type."

She stared at him. "What do you mean you have a girl-friend?" Her voice hit a high note, and she tried for a reason-able tone. "Since when?"

"Since six weeks ago."

Here she'd been feeling so warm and gooey toward him, and he'd kept this from her. She'd thought they were so close. "You've had a girlfriend for six weeks and you never mentioned it?"

He lifted his palms. "I don't tell you everything."

"You tell me everything about Checkin." It dawned on her then. Maybe he didn't tell her about his girlfriend because he thought she might have feelings for him. Gah! So freaking embarrassing. And she'd thought she'd been so careful to hide it. "Why didn't you tell me?"

He looked away and then back to her with a scowl. "Because I didn't want you to tell Mad, who'd blab it to everyone."

She crossed her arms. "I would've kept it in confidence."

"You threw me under the bus. Olivia's going to be pissed."

"Olivia who?" For some perverse reason, she wanted to hear all about the woman he'd hidden from her.

"Olivia Slater. You've probably heard of her family, they've got their hands in everything. Old money."

"I've heard of the Slater Foundation. They do a lot of good work for children in need."

"Yup. She runs it."

Dammit. She sounded like a nice person. "Is she the college girlfriend you've been pining over for years?"

He jabbed a finger at her. "That is from Mad. First of all, I didn't pine. She pined for me. Second of all, I was right not to tell you my personal shit."

She pressed her lips together, eyes watering, throat tight, really hurt that he'd hid his life from her. Even if he didn't return her lusty feelings, she'd thought at least their friendship was strong. "Is it serious?"

"Yeah," he said softly. "If things go well with our investor meetings, I'm thinking of opening an office in San Francisco. That's where she lives."

She swallowed hard, her chest tight, making it hard to breathe. He was leaving, and she hadn't had a clue. "And she's happy about this?"

He inclined his head. "She seemed to be."

"And you're happy about this?"

"It was my idea."

His casual tone pissed her off. "Here I thought we were such good friends, and I had no idea you even had a girlfriend. And now you're leaving! When were you going to tell me, huh? After you moved?"

He frowned. "Why're you so mad? I'm the one that got thrown under the bus. Now I have to deal with Olivia and, believe me, I'm going to hear it from my family. They're going to want to know why I didn't tell anyone you and I were dating for six months."

"I'm mad because I thought we were close." Her voice choked, and she didn't even try to hide her hurt, meeting his eyes directly. "You're the only one who showed up here for me."

His voice lowered, husky and coaxing. "Sabrina, come on. We are close."

"Just go to your stupid jealous girlfriend. My car's over there somewhere." She looked up and down the street, suddenly aware of a photographer with a zoom lens aimed at them. Was that her dad?

She took a step closer to the photographer. "Hey!"

The guy turned and ran away. His hair was black in a long ponytail, unlike her dad's dark blond, but definitely one of his ilk. Why would anyone want pictures of her? She couldn't possibly be that famous after one article and a TV interview. Paparazzi stalked people for pictures they could sell to the highest bidder. No one would pay a lot for her picture. Unless…was that psycho relationship counselor behind this? Did Tara Brinkman actually pay someone to dig for dirt on Sabrina? Her mind boggled at the thought.

"What's the matter?" Logan asked.

"Nothing," she replied absently, scanning the crowd to make sure the man wasn't coming back.

"An apology would be nice," Logan said, all haughty and righteous. *I was wronged, and you must apologize!*

She turned back to him and scowled. "So sorry I said you were my boyfriend. We've officially broken up. Send me a postcard from San Francisco."

He blew out a breath. "Don't be like that. I was going to tell you when I told everyone else, once I knew I could afford to make the move. I should know in a couple of weeks the way things are going to go. I still want to be friends."

Her shoulders slumped, her anger leaving her just as quickly as it had appeared. He was leaving for good, and she didn't want to end things on a sour note. This was her fault, after all. And she was putting way too much expectation on the one friend who'd come through for her. "Me too. I'm sorry I screwed things up for you. I'll talk to Olivia if you want. I'll explain it was all just a misunderstanding and nothing's going on."

He rubbed his light brown beard. "Yeah, I wish it were that easy. I'll handle it."

Her ride, a black Mercedes, pulled up and parked a short distance away.

She managed a small smile for Logan and gestured to the car. "That's my ride. Thank you for coming today."

He tugged a lock of her hair. "Shy girl rocked it."

Why did he have to leave? Her eyes welled, and she quickly turned away, hurrying to her ride.

She hadn't even made it all the way home before she got a text from Lexi saying, *What's going on?* There was a picture of her and Logan in what appeared to be an intense argument on the sidewalk, where they'd been standing not long ago. Logan was jabbing his finger at her. She had her lips pressed together, her expression clearly upset. She clicked on it, and the headline read "Trouble in Paradise?" The short article asked "Is this relationship expert not good at relationships?" Then went on to use their full names, mentioning her recent interview naming him her special someone, and then only minutes later having a serious fight with him on the sidewalk and going their separate ways.

What the hell?

Lexi texted another link a short while later. It was a celebrity gossip site and had Photoshopped pictures of her and Claire side by side. The headline read "Hollywood Love Guru." The short piece quoted an anonymous source saying Sabrina's boyfriend was related to Claire Jordan and continued with a juicy quote: "Maybe that's how Sabrina got so good at relationships, helping all those Hollywood people. Those movie stars date a lot, but only a few stick, like Claire Jordan and Jake Campbell."

Shit. This couldn't be Tara Brinkman. She wouldn't push for a positive moniker like Hollywood Love Guru. How did anyone know about the Logan-Claire connection or Sabrina's friendship with Claire for that matter? She'd never use Claire for her fame.

Her breathing was shallow, and she forced herself to calm down, closing her eyes and slowly counting backward. Okay, first things first—

Talk to Claire and explain Sabrina had nothing to do with that gossip.

Be clear with everyone that she was not a love guru of any kind and definitely not to Hollywood.

Try not to fly off to a remote desert island never to be heard from again.

4

Logan returned to work that day, wishing he could call Olivia right away, but it was too early in California. He had to talk to her before *Sunshine America* aired out there. He couldn't seem to find his focus while he worked, checking the time repeatedly, his mind drifting back to Sabrina. She'd actually gotten really worked up after the show, practically yelling at him, her eyes flashing, cheeks flushing with indignation. She hadn't seemed so porcelain doll in that moment. She'd seemed fiery and strong. Touchable, even.

Sexual compatibility was at the top of her list.

She must be *wa-a-ay* into sex.

Nope. Not going there. He was *not* going to screw things up any further with Olivia just because Sabrina tempted him one time.

Okay, technically it wasn't the first time she'd tempted him. Sometimes when he saw her talking and laughing with her friends, looking so open and warm, he'd been tempted to get closer. But as soon as he did, she went right back to reserved and quiet. Untouchable.

He raked a hand through his hair. He didn't have time for this. He had a lot of work to do.

Ben walked into his office and took a seat. His business partner and honorary brother with his short light brown hair and angular face looked tough at first glance, but his dimpled smile gave away his easygoing good humor. Ben slapped Logan's desk. "Sly bastard! All this time you said Sabrina was too sweet for you when you've been secretly dating for six months."

"Still just friends."

"Ri-i-ight." He pressed both hands to his heart and made a big fake sigh. "I saw her interview. She lit up when she saw you like she was in love with you."

She did? He shook his head. "She was just grateful a friend showed up to support her. You know how shy she is."

Ben stared at him. "I never thought she was shy."

"She blushes all the time."

"So? Some people are blushers. She has no problem talking to tons of fighting couples who walk in her door, she has a posse of close friends, and she just went on TV."

Logan thought about that. If she wasn't shy, then why did she blush so much around him?

Ben went on. "Missy says Sabrina can be downright snarky in a funny way. And coming from Missy, that's a compliment. If you're not together yet, I say go for it."

Logan barely resisted rolling his eyes. Ben had been a die-hard bachelor. They used to laugh at the guys who fell head over ass for their women. Now Ben was one of those guys. *So whipped.* Logan might be starting things up with Olivia, but you wouldn't catch him being all lovey-dovey goofy like Ben, or like Logan's brothers, or most of his friends. Geez, it was like everyone around him was getting shackled. Must be settling-down time for the old guys. He was thirty, the youngest Campbell brother, and one of the youngest of the honorary brothers he was raised with. He had no plans for marriage. He wasn't that impulsive kid he'd been in college. Now he took everything with a healthy dose of skepticism. "Wait and see" was his relationship philosophy.

Ben drummed his fingers on Logan's desk. "Sabrina laughs at all your stupid jokes. That means she's into you."

"I'm back with Olivia."

Ben straightened. "No shit?"

"Yeah. She got in touch and asked if we could reconnect. I saw her over Thanksgiving."

"That's why you've been so cheerful. I thought it was because of the investors."

"It's both."

Ben inclined his head. "Good for you. So when do I finally get to meet her?"

Ben had only heard about her, since Logan had gone to college in California and Olivia had stayed there. "Maybe sooner than you think. We'll see."

"You all set for Elias?" That was their most important investor. Logan would be meeting with him first. Only eleven days away. That meeting was on a Friday, and Logan had scheduled the rest of the meetings for the following week, hoping Elias's interest would lead to some good buzz in Silicon Valley. If Elias made an offer, the other investors would be in a frenzy to get on board with Checkin.

Logan blew out a breath. "I sure hope so."

"We'll do a dry run before you go." Ben stood. "Hey, you want to be my best man?"

Logan grinned. "I thought I already was your best man."

"You want to do it or not?"

He inclined his head. "I'd be honored. Thank you. You guys set a date?"

Ben shrugged. "Don't know. I'm leaving the planning up to Missy."

"We know who wears the pants in that family."

Ben jabbed a finger at him in mock anger and growled, "Hey, we share those pants."

Logan laughed. Ben headed out, all happy swagger. Missy was a good match for him. A true give-and-take between two equally tough people. But they could also be warm, funny, and affectionate. Olivia wasn't funny. Not that Logan needed that. He was funny enough for both of them. It was just that when he was with Ben and Missy, it was fun to watch them laughing and enjoying the hell out of each other. Whatever.

He worked until the timer on his phone chimed. Time to call Olivia. She should be at home, hopefully already caffeinated. He hit her number, and she picked up on the first ring. "Morning," she said in her smoky sexy voice.

"Morning," he said warmly. "You have your coffee?"

"Yes. I'm about to head out in a few minutes. We're having a board meeting. What's up? Are you coming out here early?" They'd already been through that. She wanted him there early; he had obligations here.

"No, I told you I've got Jake and Josh's party on Sunday. I'll be in Thursday night." His oldest brothers, identical twins, were turning thirty-five. Claire was throwing a big party for them at her and Jake's new house in Connecticut. Besides, he wanted to use every last bit of work time he had before he flew out to California.

"I know," she pouted. "I just hoped. I miss you."

"Miss you too. Listen, a friend of mine was on *Sunshine America* this morning. Funny thing, bit of a miscommunication, but somehow the host got the idea I was her boyfriend, and Sabrina agreed, being on the hot seat, but we're just friends. I just wanted—"

"Sabrina?"

"Yeah. She's a relationship counselor, and she wrote—"

"Who the hell is Sabrina?" she barked.

He pulled the phone away from his ear at her volume. "Calm down. She's just a friend."

"You have a woman friend. *You?*"

He clenched his jaw. "Yeah."

"How long have you had this, quote unquote, woman friend?"

"There's no quotes. She *is* a friend. I don't know, about six months, since we moved into this office building."

Silence.

"Olivia?"

Her voice was ice. "This is just like you, Logan. You hide stuff, you flirt with women, you flirted with my friends in college—"

"No, I was friendly. I wanted your friends to like me."

"They liked you all right. They all wanted you."

He bit back a smile. "I can't help that."

"That right there is the problem!" she screeched. "You don't take responsibility for your actions. You don't know *how* to be friendly with a woman without flirting, which is why I don't believe for one minute that Sabrina is just a friend, and the last thing…"

He tuned her out. Geez, the drama. He was surprised she hadn't outgrown it. Back in college, he'd been flattered she got so worked up over him. He'd even enjoyed all the fighting and making up. Now? Not so much.

He cut her off. "Olivia, you know how much you mean to me. Didn't I say I haven't been serious with anyone since you?" It had been eight years since their college relationship, so it sounded good and was technically true, even if the reason wasn't Olivia so much as he'd been working his ass off, no time for relationships. He hadn't exactly been celibate though.

She got quiet.

He went on. "We'll talk in person in less than two weeks. Friday night we'll have dinner, anyplace you want. I hope to have great news." That was the night after his meeting with Elias. If it went well, the possibility of moving out there would be a reality.

"Okay," she said quietly. "I'll make a reservation."

"All right, I have to get back to work."

He said bye and disconnected, troubled by Olivia's temper. It was more than jealousy. It was like she didn't trust him, and he couldn't remember ever giving her a reason to feel that way. He'd been faithful in the year they'd been together. He'd proposed, for crying out loud. She was twenty-eight now, the director of an important foundation, but she sounded like an immature college girl. She could be smooth and looked sophisticated with her sleek black hair and stunning blue eyes, her curvy body in designer clothes, but was that all just surface? Maybe he didn't know her as well as he thought he did.

His phone buzzed with a text. Olivia: *I don't want you to see Sabrina anymore.*

He blew out an exasperated breath. They worked in the

same office building, Sabrina was friends with his sister, and they knew a lot of the same people. He texted back. *We're just friends.*

If you were just friends, you would've told me about her from the beginning.

I don't care if you have guy friends.

I don't.

He went for the quickest way to reassure her. *I care about you.*

Doesn't feel like it.

I do. I'm not cheating on you, I swear.

I wish I could believe you. Frowning face emoticon.

Seriously? They were fighting by text with emoticons? He shoved his phone in his desk drawer.

He suddenly wanted Sabrina's opinion on this mess. He went downstairs to her office. It wasn't quite lunchtime yet. There were a couple of chairs in the hallway just outside her office for clients, but they were empty. He listened at the door in case she was with someone, but it was quiet. He knocked.

"Come in," she called in her professional counselor voice.

He opened the door. "Hey, you got a minute?"

"Sure!" she exclaimed from where she was sitting at her desk. She gestured him in enthusiastically. "Come on in!"

She must still be hyped up from her TV interview this morning. She didn't get up, so he went to her desk and sat on the edge of it next to her chair. The only other place to sit was across the room, and he didn't want to stand and tower over her.

Her cheeks flushed pink, and she crossed her legs and then uncrossed them.

"Does it bother you I'm sitting on your desk?" he asked. She probably preferred he sit properly on a chair, but he didn't want to holler to her from across the room. She didn't protest, so he leaned close to confide in her, catching the sweet scent of honey and flowers. "It didn't go well with Olivia."

"Oh no, I'm so sorry." Her big brown eyes were pure compassion. "I'm afraid this article might've made things worse." She handed over her phone, where there was a picture of him and Sabrina from this morning. Why was this news? The article implied Sabrina wasn't good at relationships. It did look like they were a fighting couple. He'd been mad and she'd gotten mad. Maybe they had been fighting. Had Sabrina gone toe-to-toe with him and they were still on good terms? That was the give-and-take he wanted in a relationship. Not pouting and accusations. On the other hand, maybe he shouldn't be so hard on Olivia. When you were long distance, it was hard to know what was true or not. Maybe she just needed time to learn to trust him again.

He realized Sabrina was talking. "What?"

"Which part didn't you hear?"

"I got distracted when you showed me the article."

"I said I think that psycho relationship counselor is behind this." Her eyes flashed, giving him a jolt. "She wants to discredit me."

"It'll blow over. Once the buzz dies down over your article, she'll forget about you."

"God, Logan, you really did space out on me. I also said there's a celebrity gossip piece linking me to Claire. They're calling me the Hollywood Love Guru!" Her voice rose in volume and she gestured wildly. "And Claire's cool with it! She's claimed me as her close friend and said the details of my relationship counseling are confidential. She wants me to run with it and see how far I can build my platform for this book I'm supposed to write and...and...it's insane!"

"Holy shit." It was the only possible response.

She pointed at him. "Exactly! I want the book to be big and help a lot of women, and that is the *only* reason I'm going along with all this, but it's bonkers!" She threw her hands in the air like she was tossing the whole bonkers thing away.

"All of what exactly?"

She gestured as she spoke, her color high, the most animated he'd ever seen her. He was kinda digging an animated loud Sabrina, even though she was freaking out. "My agent took that Hollywood Love Guru thing and ran with it, booking me on talk shows in LA next week! I'm beside myself. Claire's on the phone with the talk-show producers right now, making sure they know of our connection and that certain topics are off-limits. She's smoothing the way for me." She wrung her hands together. "Logan, you know I would never use Claire for her fame. Look at this article. Who could've said this? Who would've known?"

She tapped on her phone and showed him. He read the short piece and handed back her phone, his brain quickly connecting the dots. "I told the security guard at the *Sunshine America* studio my full name and that Claire Jordan was my sister-in-law. She'd put me on the list to get me backstage. Someone must've talked to him. He was just speculating on the rest of it."

She shook her head. "How can gossip from a security guard get me on the most popular talk shows?"

"Two words—Claire Jordan. And love. Okay, three words. Her name is gold, and she's such a good person she wants to let you have a little of that golden glow. It won't hurt her reputation to be linked with you, as a success story with a strong marriage."

Her eyes widened. "That's exactly what she said!"

"There you go."

She stared at him for a moment, seeming lost in thought. She took a deep breath. "Okay, leaving freak-out mode now."

He laughed.

She laughed a little too. "I'm moving my vacation up a couple of weeks to fit the talk shows in."

"Look at you, shy girl."

She blushed bright pink. "I guess I have you to thank for getting me through the first one. Now I'm on my own."

"You'll do great."

She smiled at him, a gentle warm smile that he felt in his bones. Affection, maybe even some feeling for him? He couldn't remember her ever smiling at him like that before, and now she'd done it twice. Once at the TV studio this morning when he'd first arrived backstage and now. But then her words erased any shadow of a doubt about her true feelings. "I really do feel bad about Olivia. I don't mind explaining to her the truth about that article linking us and my own part in sort of panicking in the middle of my first-ever TV show appearance and throwing you under the bus."

Sabrina was twenty-six, younger than Olivia, but so much more mature, wanting to talk the whole thing out like adults. He was sure Olivia would sooner tear Sabrina's head off than have a rational adult conversation. "No," he said. "She's the one who has to get over her issues."

"What issues?"

"Jealousy, suspicion, general mistrustfulness." He let out a breath, more wound up about Olivia than when he'd walked in here. "She's always been like this. I'll fix it when I see her in a couple of weeks."

"You sure you want to wait that long?"

He lifted one shoulder up and down. "Nothing else I can do. I already explained myself."

She pushed her chair back from her desk, and he lost her sweet scent. Worse, she crossed her legs and rested clasped hands in her lap, back to her reserved professional counselor mode. Untouchable porcelain doll. Her tone was cool and calm. "Sometimes people need to hear it more than once, maybe in a different way."

He scowled, unreasonably irritated with her help. "What different way? Sabrina is my friend. No, I'm not cheating on you. How many ways can I say that?"

Her brown eyes were full of sympathy, her tone gentle. "I hope she'll come to her senses soon. Sorry I put a wrench in the works."

He calmed down. Sabrina could always smooth the rough spots. "It's okay. Maybe things weren't as solid with Olivia as I thought. Guess I'll find out." He stood and tapped her desk. "I never told you this, but talking to you has helped me through some stuff, so thanks."

She smiled, her professional reserved smile that didn't quite reach her eyes. "That's what friends are for."

"Yeah," he muttered, turned and headed out the door. Except he'd never had a friend like her, never been able to talk to anyone like he could with her. And, for the first time, he didn't feel a weight off his shoulders when he left her office. Every step away felt difficult, plodding and heavy.

Was he really going to move to San Francisco and say goodbye to Sabrina forever? After hearing Olivia's reaction to Sabrina, he knew there was no way Olivia would understand why he wanted to keep that connection long distance. He hadn't realized until today just how much their friendship meant to him. What exactly did he hope to gain from hanging onto that connection? And what would he lose if he let her go?

5

Sabrina followed her friends into the upscale Aurora boutique in wealthy Greenport for their second weekend in a row shopping for Mad's wedding. Last Saturday they'd spent at the bridal shop for the bridal gown and bridesmaids' dresses. Today they were shopping for shoes. Mad's wedding was in June, and she wanted to get all the wedding stuff out of the way during her winter break from college. Mad had gone to college later in life and would be graduating in May at twenty-seven years old. Sabrina had graduated college young after skipping a grade in elementary school, so she'd had the exact opposite experience as Mad. She was thrilled for her all the same.

The boutique was elegant and filled with designer dresses, shoes, and purses. The air was scented with jasmine, and soft jazz piped through speakers in the ceiling. If you had money to burn, this was the place to spend it. Designer purses lined one wall, with designer shoes on the opposite wall. Hailey's mom, Brandy, worked here, and they were all getting in on her employee discount.

"Welcome, ladies!" a woman who could only be Hailey's mom exclaimed, rushing over to them. She looked like a model, tall and elegant in a royal blue close-fitting dress with an open front white bolero jacket. Her long strawberry blond hair and pale blue eyes matched Hailey's, with smooth flawless skin. "So nice to meet you all! I'm Brandy. What an exciting occasion! Congratulations again, Madison!"

Brandy hugged Mad, who hugged her back. They must've met before, since Hailey and Mad were close. Then Brandy gave Hailey a light hug and kissed the air near her cheek.

"Thanks for having us, Mom," Hailey said. She turned to the group. "Ladies, this is my mom. Mom, this is everyone." She rattled off their names, pointing at them.

"Hello!" Brandy said warmly, giving them all a wave.

"We'll just be browsing for a bit," Hailey told her mom. "I'll call you over when we're ready."

Brandy's smile stayed firmly in place, but her enthusiastic expression closed. She was probably disappointed not to be included in their group shoe shopping. "Of course," she murmured. "I'll be here."

Everyone followed Hailey over to the wall of shoes. Sabrina stopped to thank Brandy for letting them use her discount.

"Always happy to help with my daughter's wedding planning," Brandy said with a tight smile. "Enjoy yourself."

Sabrina joined her friends and glanced over her shoulder, where Hailey's mom was standing near the cushioned white settee in the center of the store watching them. Sabrina caught her eye and smiled. Brandy quickly looked away.

Hailey was busy pointing out the shoes she thought would best coordinate with their light blue bridesmaids dresses, basically white. Mad didn't care if the styles were matching as long as everyone was happy. That was Mad for you, a total tomboy, the only girl raised in a house full of older brothers and a single cop dad. She was probably Hailey's easiest bridal client ever. Mad was all *yeah, sure, whatever* to everything Hailey suggested.

Once they had shoes in hand to try on in their size, Sabrina sat on the long bench seat next to Hailey. "You look just like your mom."

Hailey huffed and looked around for her mom, who was standing a distance away. "It's so embarrassing. She tries to look like me. Her hair is naturally blond and white." She lowered her voice. "She colors it to match mine. She gets regular botox too. She used to be a model. That was like the golden time in her life. I don't think she ever got over it."

Interesting. Hailey was a former beauty queen. Her mom must've put a lot of emphasis on looks. Brandy looked young and vibrant, but she had to be at least in her forties since Hailey was twenty-seven. "How old is she?" Sabrina whispered.

"Forty-nine," Hailey whispered back. "Act your age, right?" A whimper from Hailey's pink doggie purse had Hailey leaning down to the floor and opening the top of the purse. Rose's white furry head popped up, her pink bow on top of her tiny scruff of wiry fur vibrating as she looked all around, sniffing the air, and then lay back down for a nap.

Sabrina kept her voice low. "I suppose there's no harm in looking young if it makes her feel good."

Hailey pursed her lips, but refrained from commenting further.

Someone cleared their throat loudly behind them. "Hello," a masculine voice said.

Mad popped up from the other end of the long bench, teetering in white heels. "Dad! What're you doing here?"

They all turned to look. Mr. Campbell, a retired cop, stood in the middle of racks of dresses, looking comically out of place in his faded red flannel shirt, worn jeans, and sneakers. He was tall and fit, probably in his fifties, with short brown hair that had some gray near the sides. He smiled, making his brown eyes crinkle at the corners. "I wanted to be a part of things. I couldn't make it last weekend, but Hailey said it wasn't too late for me to join in. Shoes, right?"

Mad's head whipped toward Hailey, her brown eyes wide. Hailey pasted on her beauty-queen smile. It popped up in high-stress situations.

Mr. Campbell shoved his hands in his pockets. "You don't want me here?"

Mad jerked her chin. "It's okay. I was just surprised because it's such a girl thing."

"Go back to whatever you were doing," he said, taking them all in. "Pretend I'm not here."

The women all stared, not going back to what they were doing.

He kept standing there, looking manly and uncomfortable. Sabrina thought it spoke to his love for his daughter that he would brave such a feminine outing. Finally, Hailey's mom, Brandy, walked over and greeted Mr. Campbell warmly, shaking his hand, and they had a short conversation. She must've made him feel more comfortable because he headed toward them, smiling. First he hugged Mad; then he kissed his two daughters-in-law on the cheek and raised a hand with a warm greeting for the rest of them. Finally he stopped in front of Hailey.

Hailey smiled up at him from where she sat on the bench next to Sabrina. "I wasn't sure if you'd actually show up, so I didn't mention it to Mad."

"Course I'd show." He leaned down to say in a low voice, "She's my baby. My only girl. Tell me what the mother of the bride would do. I want to fill in as best I can."

Sabrina's chest ached. What a great dad, doing his best to take the place of an absentee mom.

Hailey gave him a soft smile. "Something needs doing, Mr. Campbell, I'll let you know."

Mr. Campbell straightened. "Please call me Joe. You ladies are like sisters to Mad. I've never been involved in planning a wedding. What can I do to help?"

Hailey gave his forearm a squeeze. "I appreciate the offer, Joe, but, honestly, almost everything is taken care of at this point."

Joe pulled a folded check out of his front shirt pocket and handed it to Hailey. "I know it's not much, but I want to help. I had this saved for her college tuition, but Mad insisted it was covered. Put this to whatever she needs."

Hailey unfolded the check. Five thousand dollars. Not enough to cover four years of college tuition, but a nice contribution toward the wedding. "Thank you."

Joe spoke in a conspiratorial tone. "At first I thought Jake helped her out with tuition, but then I found out it was Josh."

Hailey stiffened. "Josh?" Her nemesis had done something good. Would this make Hailey soften toward him?

Joe nodded. "Put off his own dream of owning a bar to do it."

"I had no idea," Hailey whispered, glancing down the row of women to Mad and back to Joe. "Mad never said anything."

Joe touched his index finger to his temple. "My kids think I don't see, but I do. I know what's up with every one of them. That's what made me a good cop. I'm observant."

"Hey, Dad!" Mad called. "What do you think of these?" She wore shiny white high-heeled boots that went up to her knees. Kind of a weird choice to go with a wedding gown, but Mad had an unusual take on women's fashion, which was to say no clue at all.

Hailey frowned, but didn't immediately reject the choice. She was a very diplomatic wedding planner.

"If you like them, I like them," Joe said.

"I like them," Mad said, looking down at them and smiling.

Hailey rushed over to talk to Mad and then gestured to Brandy to join them. Next thing you knew, Mad was seated on the bench with a whole row of bride-appropriate shoes to try on.

The rest of them had a great time trying on shoes, stopping frequently to give Mad a thumbs-up or thumbs-down for whatever she tried on. Her dad wasn't much help. He just wanted her to be happy, so he agreed with whatever she liked. The rest of them wanted her to be happy *and* look good.

Once Sabrina had chosen her bridesmaid shoes, a practical white pump with a small embroidered daisy on the side, she browsed the gorgeously impractical shoes just for fun. She fondled a silver metallic leather stiletto. It was breathtaking. Open-toed with four sets of metallic silver wings running up the front, two ankle straps. Wearing something like this said

I'm ready to soar. If she was going to face down all those cameras and lights, she'd be doing it with wings on her feet.

She held them up to her friends. "What do you think for my talk-show interviews in LA?" She'd texted her friends about her big LA moment as soon as she'd heard.

"Yes!" Hailey exclaimed. "How much are they?"

Sabrina checked the price and winced. "Too much."

"I'll chip in," Hailey said.

"We'll all chip in," Lexi said, gesturing for the others to join in.

The ladies insisted.

Sabrina shook her head. "I appreciate it. Really. But I got it." She was doing well in her practice and hoped to have even more clients after all the publicity. Fingers crossed the rest of her interviews went as smoothly as her *Sunshine America* interview. Besides, she lived modestly in a one-bedroom apartment. She stayed there mostly because her close friends lived in the same building. Though now only Lexi was left since her other two close friends, Missy and Ally, had moved in with their fiancés. A pang of pure envy hit. When she'd first joined the Happy Endings Book Club, it had been designed as a singles book club. No men had ever stuck around, though, and they'd become a tight sisterhood of single women united in their love of romance novels.

But now things were very different. Nearly everyone had found their special someone. It was just her, Hailey, and Lexi left in the singles department. Totally unfair, now that she thought about it. She could understand Lexi being single, the woman was so jaded about men, but Sabrina and Hailey had dedicated their lives to relationships. How was it that neither of them had one? Were they just too close to all of the issues that could pop up to take a chance? Too caught up in helping other couples to invest time in their own love lives? She should have a heart-to-heart with Hailey and get to the bottom of this. It had never seemed such a glaring problem before, but with all the attention on Sabrina's supposed relationship expertise, it was a real issue.

Hailey sighed. "We just feel bad we can't go out to LA

with you. It's such a shame you and Claire are just missing each other." Sabrina was heading out to California two days after Claire moved to Connecticut permanently. Claire and her husband, Jake, were arriving tonight at their new house.

Sabrina ran a finger over one of her new shoes' wings. "I'll see her tomorrow at Jake and Josh's birthday party. I'm going over a little early to raid her closet and get some coaching. She knows all the talk-show hosts."

Lexi stood, looking right at Sabrina, her brown eyes gleaming with mischief. "You did great on *Sunshine America* with Logan there."

Sabrina shot her a dark look. *Ha-ha, keep it up. Next guy you talk to will be fair game for harassing the hell out of you.*

Lexi winked. "And things got pretty heated on the sidewalk between you two."

"I explained that," Sabrina said through her teeth. Though the story her friends had heard was that Logan was mad she'd pretended he was her boyfriend. She was especially careful what she shared around Mad, who'd surely pass along any juicy tidbits to Logan. Only Lexi knew the truth. Sabrina had spilled her guts on the drive over here with Lexi, confessing she really liked Logan so much more than a friend, despite every practical reason she shouldn't, including the pertinent fact that he had a girlfriend and was moving to San Francisco. Lexi had informed Sabrina that they'd all been hopeful for her to get together with Logan, but had believed her when she said they were just friends. Only Mad hadn't been hopeful, convinced Logan was stuck on his ex. Too bad Mad was the one who was right. Sabrina still swore Lexi to secrecy because she didn't want her one-sided longing for Logan to get back to him. Also Logan hadn't yet told his friends and family about his move. Everything hinged on his investor meetings.

Lexi blew her a kiss.

Sabrina scowled. Sometimes Lexi's sensitivity level was on par with a guy's. Not that all men were like that, but the vast majority Sabrina encountered in her practice were oblivious to sensitive issues. Just like her clueless ex. Not only had

Kevin sent her a wedding invitation—her! His jilted bride! He'd followed up with an enthusiastic email, telling her how wonderful his fiancée was and how he really wanted Sabrina to meet her. The man had no clue about boundaries or her emotional state. It suddenly occurred to her that it was a blessing she hadn't married Kevin. Clearly his cluelessness hadn't improved over the years. It would've worn at her, small slights and bigger wounds that he wouldn't have noticed.

Joe cocked his head. "Logan was on TV?"

Logan. He wasn't clueless at all. He'd been there for her during her TV appearance, reading between the lines to the fear under her bravado. Her heart cracked open, feeling so much more than lust for him. Her brain knew better; her heart didn't care.

Sabrina turned to Joe. "He was backstage." Her cheeks heated, and she willed herself to stop blushing. Joe studied her intently, showing his wily cop ways, and she cracked under the pressure. "He showed up to cheer me on."

One corner of his mouth lifted, reminding her of Logan's amused smile. "Is that right?"

Lexi added fuel to the fire, informing Joe, "He drove all the way to the city at an ungodly hour on a Monday." She thumped her chest. "Above and beyond, A for effort."

Joe's brows went up, staring at Lexi, but he said nothing. What was there to say? Lexi made it sound like Logan had a thing for her. Joe's attention returned to Sabrina, and she felt the telltale blush spread to her neck.

"We're good friends," she assured him.

Mad piped up. "Yeah. Logan's still stuck on whatsher-name from college."

"Olivia," Sabrina supplied.

"Since when?" Joe asked.

Mad stood, back to wearing her usual black work boots. "Since forever, Dad. Everyone knows."

Joe's brows scrunched together.

"I only recently heard about her," Sabrina offered, trying

to make Joe feel better for being out of the loop. "I think he likes to keep his private life private."

"Then how'd I know?" Mad asked.

Hailey distracted Mad, taking Rose out of her doggie purse and handing her over for cuddles. Mad had taken care of Rose right before they all gave Hailey the little dog as a present, so they had a special bond. Rose was part of an intervention Sabrina had orchestrated for Hailey on New Year's Eve, trying to help her slow down from the hyper speed she'd latched onto after she'd ended her long-term friends-with-benefits arrangement. The real stressor for Hailey, in Sabrina's professional opinion, was losing her sparring partner in Josh when he'd become involved with the beautiful bohemian Clarissa just as Hailey became single. Swing and a miss for Hailey, though she'd never admit it.

Joe looked to Sabrina, his brow crinkled. "Logan was with her eight years ago. How could he be hung up that long?"

"They reconnected recently," Sabrina said. She looked away, her eyes hot. She'd been lucky to have Logan in her life for the short time that she had, and now he was leaving. Her throat tightened, eyes stinging, heart *aching*. She gave herself a moment to acknowledge her loss. It was time for her to let go of Logan.

She had to look to the future, to her career, to her upcoming book and helping so many women. That was where she should focus all of her energy. She stood, holding up her shoes, and forced some cheer into her voice. "Brandy, I'll take these."

Brandy smiled and gestured for her to follow her to the counter.

Once they'd all paid for the shoes, with an employee discount courtesy of Brandy, they headed for their next stop —lunch. Hailey had made reservations in a private room of an Italian restaurant nearby.

"Joe, you're welcome to join us for lunch," Hailey said. "I'm sure the restaurant could add one more to the reservation."

Joe smiled. "Thanks, but I have to go. You ladies enjoy yourselves."

Mad gave him a hug. "Thanks for coming. Not every day your daughter is a bride, huh?"

Joe's eyes misted and he ruffled Mad's hair. She scowled and smoothed it out. "You're a beautiful bride, Mad. Couldn't be more proud."

Mad's lips twisted to the side, her own eyes misting. "See ya."

They all headed out the door, except Joe, who turned and went back to the counter. Sabrina stopped in front of the door and peeked over her shoulder. Joe was talking to Brandy, the pair of them showing all the classic flirtation signals. Joe standing tall, shoulders thrown back. Brandy smiling, looking away and back. Whoa.

Sabrina went out the door and stopped her friends on the sidewalk outside. "You guys, look."

They peered through the large picture window as Brandy handed Joe her business card.

"Omigod," Hailey whispered. "What just happened?"

"Bah," Mad said. "He's probably going to surprise me with a wedding present. Your mom's probably going to pick out a purse or something for him."

"I think he asked her out," Sabrina said.

Joe turned, heading their way, a big smile on his face.

They all quickly turned from the window, acting casual, though none of them could think of a single thing to say.

Joe stepped outside, whistling, turned and walked down the sidewalk away from them. He hadn't even noticed them gawking.

"What just happened!" Hailey exclaimed, staring at Joe's retreating back.

"Maybe we'll end up sisters," Mad said, a hint of longing in her voice.

Sabrina suppressed a laugh. That would make Josh—Hailey's nemesis—her brother. Ever since their paid-wedding-date fiasco, Hailey had been demanding her money back while Josh kept telling her to go back to his place and get it. Which, of course, they all knew was code for some private time. Their sexual chemistry was off the charts. So was their hostility. Brother and sister! Hysterical!

"Omigod!" Hailey exclaimed at the top of her lungs, staring at her mom. Rose's head popped out of Hailey's dog purse, ears perked for trouble.

Sabrina gently nudged Hailey away from the window and down the sidewalk. Whatever was about to happen between Joe and Brandy, they didn't need Hailey for it.

6

———

Sabrina showed up at Claire and Jake's new home two hours early for her special Claire coaching session for the LA interviews and was glad she had because she got to see their new place in the lingering sunlight. Gorgeous! She pulled into the circular driveway of the main house, a stone and stucco mansion with arts-and-crafts-style post and beams on the upper levels and the large porch. This place was so much more than a horse farm. It was a freaking estate. She'd passed another smaller house after she'd driven through the main gate, and Claire had told her there was another historic home, dating from the eighteen hundreds, on the property. Acres of rolling hills surrounded the home with woodlands just beyond. The landscape was stark in January with patches of melting snow and the trees without leaves, but she could imagine how amazing it would look in the bloom of spring, the vibrant life of summer, and the gorgeous color of a Connecticut fall.

She got out of her car, spotting brown horses with thick gray blankets over their backs grazing in a large grassy paddock near a pond. There was a riding ring in the distance, two barns, stables, and who knew what else! Claire and Jake could well afford it. She was an A-list movie star, and Jake was a billionaire on his own through his tech company.

It was so incredibly luxurious she suddenly felt under-dressed in her black and white striped sweater, black pants, and black flats. She should've worn a dress, definitely heels, and spent more time on her makeup. She blew out a breath. She was being silly. This was down-to-earth Claire.

She headed to the front door and rang the bell, the sound echoing inside the place. The door opened a few minutes later to Claire, back to her natural blond shoulder-length hair, dressed casually in a white blouse, oversized beige cardigan, faded jeans with holes in the knees, and beige moccasins on her feet. Her hazel eyes lit up at the sight of Sabrina, and she threw her arms wide. "You made it! Come in, come in!"

Sabrina stepped inside, immediately put at ease by Claire's warmth. She hugged her friend. Claire had joined the Happy Endings Book Club more than two years ago when she first started filming the Fierce trilogy in Connecticut. The author of the Fierce trilogy, Julia Marino, had been a member at the time. Claire had connected with their little group and hadn't let go since. Sabrina knew Claire appreciated having friends who weren't in the movie industry; she often said she felt used by the people she met. Then, of course, once Claire got together with Jake Campbell, she was hooked for good since Jake's sister, Mad, was part of the book club. The web of relationships between the Happy Endings Book Club and the Campbell family with their honorary brothers had become sticky, engagements and marriages popping up on a regular basis. For *some* of them, anyway. Not that Sabrina was bitter or anything. It really hadn't bothered her before everyone started calling her a relationship expert. Ugh. At some point she had to stop feeling like a fraud, right?

Claire pulled away, smiling her perfect white-toothed smile. "You want the tour first or clothes?"

Sabrina took off her black wool jacket and looked around the large formal foyer. The walls were done in shades of gold like an Italian fresco painting, and two large framed paintings that resembled sunlight with a weird pattern of jagged black hung on opposite walls. In the center of the foyer was a large round wood pedestal table with a carved wooden bowl on top of it. A crystal chandelier hung above. The floor was a warm dark hardwood with a crosshatch pattern. The whole thing screamed luxury, and that was just the foyer! "Tour."

"You got it." Claire hung up Sabrina's coat in a nearby hall closet.

"Where's Frank?" That was Claire's bodyguard.

"He's in the private apartment over the detached garage. Don't worry. He's got the guest list and monitors out the wazoo. He's the one that buzzed you through the gate. Come on." She gestured for Sabrina to follow and led her out of the foyer to a huge room with a soaring ceiling leading all the way up to the post and beams of the roof. "Living room."

"Wow," Sabrina breathed. The fireplace was massive with a two-story white and light gray limestone front. The center of the room featured a seating area with several white sofas and beige floral-patterned chairs with wood trim. The opposite wall from the fireplace held a large white entertainment center flanked by bookcases and glass cabinets.

"You know I had to have my books!" Claire gestured to them. She was a big reader like all of them.

Sabrina's eye caught on the black wrought-iron rail of a loft overlooking the living room.

"Ooh!" Claire exclaimed. "You'll love the loft. It's so cozy."

Sabrina followed her up a spiral staircase to the loft with more white sofas and beige chairs. The view from up here through the huge windows of the living room to the rest of the estate was spectacular.

"You want something to drink?" Claire asked, gesturing to a wet bar housed in a rich dark cherrywood cabinet.

"Sure."

"White wine okay?"

"Absolutely."

"Claire!" Jake boomed. "Where are you? I can't find my sneakers."

Claire leaned over the railing overlooking the living room. "Sabrina's here. Try to sound civilized."

A few moments later, Jake was in the loft with them. He

looked exactly like his twin, Josh, tall with an athletic grace, dark brown hair and eyes, except his hair was always neatly trimmed. Josh let his hair grow long enough that it curled a bit at the nape of his neck. Jake had some dark stubble on his square jaw; his smile flashed white. A handsome man by any measure. Not as handsome as his brother Logan…*Oh, no, we are not going there.*

Sabrina gave him a little wave. "Hi, Jake. Happy birthday!"

"Hey, Sabrina, thanks. Great to see you again." He crossed to her and gave her a hug. "I'm hearing amazing things are in the works for you."

"Yeah, I'm a little nervous."

"Claire will get you all set. And if you get rattled, just picture them in their underwear." He winked.

Claire grinned. "That never worked for me because I just start laughing."

Jake turned to Claire. "Any guesses on the sneakers?" He was barefoot in jeans and a long-sleeved light blue button-down shirt.

Claire turned to Sabrina. "Our personal stuff arrived yesterday, and half of it's still in boxes." She turned back to Jake. "Try the man cave."

Jake narrowed his eyes. "Why is your entire wardrobe all nicely hung up and laid out in our closet and my stuff is in boxes in the basement?"

Claire slung an arm over Sabrina's shoulders. "Because I knew we were doing a wardrobe fitting today."

Jake grumbled something, turned, and left. A pair of gray socks stuck out of his back jeans pocket.

"Love you!" Claire cooed after him.

"Love you too!" he hollered from somewhere downstairs.

Claire smiled dreamily before getting a couple of wine-glasses and pouring them some wine. She gestured for Sabrina to take a seat on the white sofa. "Okay if I show you more of the tour later? I'd like to catch up."

"Of course."

Claire handed Sabrina her wine and took a seat next to

her. "It's all pretty much like this. Limestone and fieldstone fireplaces in the living areas, lots of neutral white and beige furniture. The upstairs is mostly empty except for the master bedroom. We'll probably spend most of the party in the man cave—" she waved a hand in the air "—big screen TV, bar, pool table, Ping-Pong, some arcade games and pinball. His stuff is lined up along the back wall, out of the way. It's Jake's dream room basically, but on the other side of that is my favorite feature—a wine cellar with a tasting room."

"Wow!"

Claire crossed one leg over the other, looking sophisticated despite her casual attire. "That was already here; the previous owners were huge wine aficionados. Anyway, most of what you see was either left from the previous owners or from the designer we hired to make everything comfortable but neutral. We'll go ahead and add some personal touches after we live here for a while. Some art and framed pictures, stuff like that." She took a sip of wine. "I kept my place in California. Jake sold his. Actually, Logan's going to be staying at my place when he goes out for his meetings this week."

Sabrina's shoulders drooped at the mention of Logan. She had to let go of him, she knew that, but every cell in her being protested. Throat suddenly tight, she took a sip of wine to ease it.

Claire looked at her expectantly. Clearly she wanted to hear more about the Logan situation. Claire knew Logan had showed up at *Sunshine America* to support Sabrina, and she knew about the news story that made it sound like they were having a lovers' quarrel on the sidewalk. Not to mention Claire had a real soft spot for her brothers-in-law and sister-in-law, always trying to help them out and make sure they were happy. She did the same for her friends, but that tie by marriage to the Campbells brought out her protective side.

Claire leaned close. "What's the deal with Logan? You two—"

"Just friends," Sabrina said firmly.

"Why?" She lowered her voice. "I never said this, but he's seriously hot. And take it from someone on the inside with the Campbell family, he's probably the most easygoing guy there. Unlike some hardheaded men."

Sabrina laughed. "Jake is not hardheaded. He's sweet."

Claire shook her head, smiling. "Oh, we've gone a round or two. We're both hardheaded."

"But you talk it through."

Claire bit back a smile. "Sometimes." Her voice dropped, husky and suggestive. "Sometimes it works out in other interesting ways."

A pang of jealousy made Sabrina clench her teeth. She wished she were above it, but there it was. Claire and Jake's love was palpable. They were married with a beautiful home, and Claire had told her before they were trying to get pregnant. Meanwhile, Sabrina was stuck in the friend zone.

"Here's the problem with Logan," Sabrina declared much too loudly. She was getting worked up all over again.

Claire's eyes widened. "Do tell."

She stared at her wine and said in a small voice, "I screwed everything up."

"Come on, it can't be that bad."

She lifted her head. "I've been friends with him for six months, secretly lusting after him—"

"I knew it!" Claire crowed. "I told Jake there was no way it was platonic."

"Do not breathe a word of this to Jake."

Claire quickly mimed zipping her lips.

Sabrina sighed. "I never let him know because I thought he was a commitment-phobe. He never got serious with anyone; he never even mentioned a date. I have a real thing against commitment-phobes, you know?"

Claire nodded vigorously, her lips still zipped shut.

"And I thought he was a little impulsive, a risk taker. I mean because he left a good job with Jake to start his own company. A safe stable job for a start-up. They almost always fail. He had to sleep on Ben's sofa for a whole year." Ben had kept his full-time job that first year, only working nights and weekends with Logan, whose work was the basis of their entire company. "But now I'm thinking I got it all wrong. He's got this amazing stable family and all those honorary brothers, so that would've mitigated the risk of starting his own business, you know? He had support." She smacked her forehead. "Jake probably would've given Logan his old job back if Checkin failed."

Claire nodded, her gaze sympathetic.

It suddenly occurred to her that Logan remaining loyal to his college girlfriend also showed signs of risk aversion. He hadn't chanced another serious relationship, staying with what he knew had worked. And his immense commitment to Checkin made him seem much more stable than she'd first thought. How could she have gotten it so wrong?

Sabrina sucked in air, gesturing wildly. "My diagnosis was completely off base, and now it's too late!"

Claire raised a hand. "I gotta say—"

Sabrina was on a roll. "I built up this idea in my mind of why Logan was definitely not relationship material. Maybe because I feared he wasn't into me like I was into him lust-wise and now so much more, you know?" She glanced at Claire, who was smiling with her lips still sealed. "I don't know why I was so far off. I'm usually much more insightful. Maybe lust interfered with my thinking. But then he does this amazing thing showing up for me on *Sunshine America*, the only one to show up for me—"

"I wanted to—"

"I know. It was a tough time and location for anyone to show up for, but he did, and I just opened up inside, you know?" She placed her palm over her heart. "Like all warm and gooey. And then and then..." Her voice choked.

"What?"

She guzzled some wine. "He's involved in a long-distance relationship with his college girlfriend. That he never mentioned! He kept it all to himself, even though we talk every freaking week! And I don't mean a passing hello, I mean we sit down, have lunch, and really talk. He's planning on moving to San Francisco permanently to be with her if the investor meetings go well, which I'm sure they will. He's leaving and he never said shit!"

"Omigod, he's moving for a woman!" Claire set her glass down on a nearby end table. "Jake didn't know any of this or I would've known. I can't believe Logan kept his relationship from everyone. When did they get back together?"

"Six weeks ago, well, I guess it's seven weeks now." Sabrina swallowed hard. "I thought we were so close. Now he's leaving, and I missed my chance."

Claire gave her a sympathetic look. "Honey, I'm so sorry. I had no idea he had that stuff going on."

Sabrina nodded. "I screwed things up for him too. I feel terrible about it."

"What'd you do?" Claire asked eagerly.

"I didn't know about his girlfriend, so after I implied he was my boyfriend on TV, she got really mad. He says she's the jealous type, even though he explained we were just friends. And there was that article that looked like we were fighting, which made it sound like we were having a lovers' spat."

"Ha! You? The most calm, composed, kickass communicator on the planet had a breakdown in communication with the most easygoing guy on the planet? Ridiculous! I'm sure if you actually were a couple, you'd talk everything through without even raising your voices."

Sabrina pressed her lips together. It sure hadn't gone down that way. "Yeah, well, he was pretty mad I implied he was my boyfriend." She huffed. "And I was legit mad he'd hidden this important part of his life from me."

Claire slashed a hand through the air. "That is it. She's out; you're in."

Her head jerked back. "Claire, you can't break them up."

Claire's eyes flashed. "I don't like her."

"You've never met her."

Claire ticked off Olivia's sins on her fingers. "She's jealous, mistrustful, unforgiving. Nope. Not for my little brother."

Sabrina laughed. "Little brother? He's only a year younger than you."

"Don't care." She eyed Sabrina's outfit. "Come on, let's go to my closet. I've got something in mind for you for tonight plus some summery clothes for your interviews in LA." Claire was a little shorter than Sabrina, but her clothes still fit. Although some of the dresses ended a little high on Sabrina's legs.

Sabrina stared at Claire in her super-casual outfit. "Why do I have to change for tonight? Do I look underdressed for the party? You're dressed casual."

"I'll change too." She smiled mischievously. "Besides, you're not underdressed enough for what I have in mind. We're going to unbutton you a bit, make you more approachable."

"For what?" Realization dawned. "Don't you dare say anything to Logan."

"I won't have to. Your smoking hot bod will do all the talking for me."

She glanced down at herself with her modest curves. "Err..."

Claire leaned in. "Did you ever stop to think why Logan didn't make a move on you first? You've been friends with him for six months, and he only connected with Olivia a little over a month ago. Believe me, the Campbell men won't hesitate to move in on a woman, but they need a clear signal."

A smile played over her lips, and she leaned back. "When I first got together with Jake, Hailey had told me he needed an affirmation of desire and consent before he'd make a move." She laughed. "Later, he said that was what Josh had told Hailey to tell me, just messing with her, and then the twins switched places, so I said it to Jake. Omigod! I laughed so hard when I found out, because it was so awkward. I'm all like, 'Here's my affirmation of desire and consent. Let's have sex.' And Jake's all like, 'Huh? Okay.'" She waved that away. "Anyway, the Campbell men have been raised to be gentlemen, to treat women like they'd want their little sister to be treated, with care and respect. So if Logan didn't make a move on you, it's either because he wasn't interested or he didn't get a clear signal from you."

Her stomach did a jittery dance, her pulse quickening. A

small ray of hope brightened her gloom over losing him. Then she came to her senses. "What about Olivia?"

Claire lifted a palm. "We're not going to do anything but put out a clear signal. Just a subtle test of potential interest."

Sabrina shook her head, her role as a relationship counselor bringing her back to reality. "No. Claire, this goes against everything I stand for. I would never get between a couple."

Claire smiled brightly. "That's great. Make sure you tell him how much you want him to work things out with Olivia. If he's interested in you, that will be a problem for him."

Sabrina rubbed her temple. "I don't know. This feels tricky somehow."

"You want to wave goodbye to him, never knowing?"

She didn't want to say goodbye to him at all. She downed her wine in one swallow and nodded at Claire, who beamed. She followed her downstairs on shaky legs, hoping she wasn't about to make a complete fool of herself.

7
———

Sabrina wore a white dress. In a sea of black and dark winter colors at Jake and Josh's birthday party, she stood out like lightning in a dark sky. Nothing particularly revealing about the dress, yet Logan couldn't tear his gaze away. The top went up to her neck and ended modestly at her knees. It was sleeveless, so her shoulders and arms were exposed. Bare legs too, her slender feet in open-toed white sandals. What was it that was different? Her dark blond hair was down, soft waves brushing her shoulders. Her brown eyes looked smoky with dark liner, her lips painted rosy pink. More makeup than usual, but still Sabrina. His gaze took another tour of her dress. The rows of silver and gold crystals diagonally across the top reversed direction below her waist past her hips, drawing his eye to the swell of her breasts, her small waist, the curve of her hips. The combined effect was nothing short of stunning.

She looked confident, powerful, insanely sexy. He could not stop staring at her curves. So was Marcus, the lech. His close friend and honorary brother stood at his side at the bar in Jake's new man cave. Sabrina was just across the way, standing next to Lexi near the pool table.

"Damn," Marcus said under his breath, "Sabrina cleans up good." Marcus was not the guy you wanted to stand next to at a party—if you were a guy—because you'd only look homely next to him. He was nobody's wingman. He looked like he'd just stepped out of a cologne ad or something. Black close-cropped hair, dark eyes with thick lashes, tanned skin, and chiseled cheekbones. At least his nose had been broken, so he wasn't perfect. He worked out much harder than necessary, with the overly muscled arms to show for it.

"Don't talk about her like that," Logan snapped.

"What's your problem?"

"She's my friend."

"I wanna be her friend too." Marcus socked his arm and swaggered over to Sabrina. Dammit. Marcus was such a hulk, tall and wide, that he completely blocked Logan's view of Sabrina. He was pretty sure Sabrina didn't care about big muscles. Actually, he didn't know what she liked in a guy. He'd never seen her flirting, never saw her with a guy.

He took a pull on his beer, watching as Marcus leaned down, probably smiling at her, flirting like he always did. Logan clenched his jaw. He was not going to come off like some jealous boyfriend walking over there and telling Marcus to get lost. He endured several excruciating minutes of Marcus's flirting, and then Marcus and Sabrina walked away together. Lexi started playing pool with some of the guys.

He caught the rear view of Sabrina, the silver and gold crystals in straight lines down her back pointing like arrows to the sweetest curve of ass he'd ever seen. How had he missed that before? Wait. Where were they going? Upstairs? Was Marcus taking her upstairs for some privacy? Everyone else was hanging out in the man cave.

He set his beer down on the bar and followed them, keeping back a distance. They went around the corner and down a ramp, the light dimmer here, the air cooler. Sabrina was laughing at something Marcus said as they walked through an arched brick hallway. He couldn't hear Marcus's low voice. What the hell was he up to?

Logan couldn't stand it anymore. "Hey, Sabrina. Where you headed?"

She whirled. "Hi! I was telling Marcus about the wine-tasting room. He says he knows all about wine, so we're going to check it out." Marcus owned his own bar in the city, The Burrow. Logan didn't know anything about wine. He was a beer man.

"Would you like to join us?" Sabrina asked.

He instantly felt better. "Sure," he said, catching up with them. "What's with the dress?"

"Smooth," Marcus muttered. "You look beautiful, Sabrina."

Sabrina blushed prettily and smiled up at Marcus. "Thank you." She looked at Logan, her smile dropping. "What do you mean what's with the dress?"

"I don't know. It just seems really dressy for a birthday party."

"What're you, the fashion police?" Marcus asked with a laugh. "Might want to upgrade from jeans and sneakers, then." Marcus dressed like a city metrosexual in crisp shirts, tailored pants, and dress shoes. He could be casual in jeans and sneakers like the rest of the normal men in the world, but tonight he was Mr. Metrosexual in a light blue shirt and dark gray pants. Logan was in his usual long-sleeved cotton shirt, jeans, and, yes, sneakers. Now that he saw Sabrina dressed to kill, he kinda wished he'd stepped it up a notch.

Logan shot Marcus a dark look before telling Sabrina, "It's a nice dress."

"Thanks," she said. No smile for him. It was on the tip of his tongue—you look stunning, insanely sexy—but he stopped himself. They were friends and he had a girlfriend. Kinda. The long-distance thing with Olivia made it hard to know where he stood, but she'd seemed really into a future together. He'd find out in less than a week when he took her to dinner. *Wait and see, wait and see.*

The hallway ended in a room with a glossy honey-colored semicircle bar with five red velvet chairs set around it. Long cushioned benches lined opposite walls. Four hanging lights over the bar spotlighted his twin brothers, Jake and Josh, serving up drinks. Josh was pouring wine for their sisters-in-law while Jake was pouring what looked like scotch for their brothers.

The way to tell the twins apart was easy if you knew them well, because they were complements of each other. Josh was laid-back and dressed casually in flannel shirts, faded T-shirts, and ripped jeans, letting his hair grow shaggy, forgetting to shave for days on end. Jake was driven, dressed in crisp designer clothes—even his casual clothes were designer—his hair always cut and styled, sometimes stubbled, but usually clean-shaven. They had a similar sense of humor, though, loving to razz people. Feisty banter with a woman was foreplay to them.

Maybe Logan should explain that to Hailey, who took everything Josh said so personally. Josh would kill him if he did. Whatever. If Josh wanted to torture himself by never getting Hailey out of his system, then that was his own damn fault.

Marcus slipped behind the bar. "All right, which one of you birthday boys wants a break? I got this."

His sister-in-law Claire leaned across the bar and spoke in her throaty voice. "Josh, could you grab some of those champagne bottles and take them to the other bar? My friends love champagne."

"Sure." Josh reached under the bar and pulled two bottles of champagne out. "For my birthday, eh?"

"Sure," Claire said with a laugh. "Honestly, they don't need a reason."

Josh nodded once and left. Marcus took over with the wine.

Jake shook his head at Claire, smiling. "Subtle."

Claire smiled mischievously. "I know." Probably Hailey liked champagne.

"C'mere, you," Claire said, crooking her finger at Sabrina, who was setting her purse on one of the long benches across the room. "You can have my seat. I think I've tasted enough wine. I'm going to bring some of the food down."

His sisters-in-law jumped up to help Claire, and the three of them headed out. He watched while Claire stopped next to

Sabrina on her way out, giving her shoulder a squeeze and whispering something. Sabrina laughed, saying something to her friends he couldn't quite catch, all warm, friendly smiles. Now why couldn't Sabrina be warm and open like that with him? It was like he made her close up just by being near. The exact opposite effect he usually had on women.

Logan casually waited for Sabrina to take a seat at the bar before taking the seat next to her. "All set for LA?"

She nodded at Marcus, who was holding up a bottle of red to her, before answering Logan. "Yeah. Claire lent me three outfits, and I already had one of my own that I was happy with. I got these kickass shoes with wings—"

"Wings?" Logan asked. "Like a superhero or something?"

She giggled. Sabrina never giggled. "Just a minute. I'll show you." She walked over to the cushioned bench and bent to retrieve her phone from her purse. He admired her fine ass again and quickly looked away as soon as she straightened. He caught Marcus's knowing look. Jake chuckled.

Logan stared straight ahead, working on being the picture of innocence.

Sabrina sat next to him and showed him her phone with a picture of the shoes. "Aren't they gorgeous?" Silver stilettos with wings and ankle straps. Sexy as hell. Who was this woman, and what had she done with untouchable porcelain-doll Sabrina?

"What's going on with you?" he asked, genuinely confused. "The whole time I've known you, you're dressed like a professional, like some kind of…" He gestured up and down her sexy body, trying to think of something more complimentary than untouchable porcelain doll.

She took a sip of the small bit of wine Marcus set in front of her for tasting. "Like a counselor?"

Logan pointed at her. "Yes! And now you're suddenly wearing stuff you'd see on the red carpet. Claire stuff. Are you trying to be like Claire?"

"Have some scotch," Jake said, shoving a tumbler in front of him. "Don't talk so much."

He glared at his big brother.

Sabrina smiled at Marcus. "This is delicious wine. Hints of chocolate in it. What's it called?"

Marcus lifted the bottle. "Decadence."

Sabrina licked her lips, and Logan's cock perked up. "I love Decadence," she purred.

"Have some more," Marcus said, filling her glass.

"Oh, stop, stop!" Sabrina said with a laugh. "I started the party early with Claire. This is my third glass." She leaned close and batted her eyes at Marcus. "Can you tell?"

Marcus leaned close, nose to nose, his voice husky. "Not at all, darlin'. Enjoy your wine."

Sabrina patted Marcus's clean-shaven cheek. He caught her hand and kissed the palm. Sabrina took her hand back and stared at it.

Logan tossed back some scotch. He winced, not used to hard liquor. Jake was watching him closely for some reason. Logan glanced over to his brothers, Alex and Ty, sitting on his other side to see if they were watching him too, but they were still deep in conversation about kid stuff. They were both dads.

He turned back to Sabrina, feeling Jake's eyes on him. What was with Jake today? "So you got the clothes and the shoes. You all set for the hard-hitting interview questions?"

"We'll see," Sabrina caroled. He'd honestly never seen her like this, all giggly and practically singing her words.

"Are you drunk?" If she was drunk, he should probably get her home before she did something stupid like hook up with Marcus. His friend was a great guy, just not great at relationships. Sabrina deserved better than that.

She gave him a goofy smile and sipped her red wine. "Wouldn't you like to know?"

Jake and Marcus exchanged a look behind the bar, grinning at each other, clearly finding Sabrina entertaining. Logan didn't see what was so funny.

"Yeah, I would like to know," Logan said. "That's why I asked."

She let out a soft sigh and set her glass on the bar with a thunk. She turned to him, her eyes wide, her voice earnest.

"Logan, I'm really, really sorry I threw you under the bus, and I just want you to know I really, so sincerely hope you can work things out with Olivia. Okay?" She didn't wait for a response, instead answering her own question. "Okay. Good talk."

"Thanks."

She cocked her head. "Is that a problem for you?"

His brows scrunched together in confusion. He had no idea what she was talking about.

"Olivia?" Jake asked. "The one from college?"

Sabrina chugged her wine.

"Yeah, we reconnected recently," Logan said, tearing his gaze from Sabrina. "You know, it's long distance, she's out in San Francisco, so I didn't tell anyone about it. Kind of wait and see where things go."

"I remember her from your graduation," Jake said. "High-strung."

"She's not high-strung," Logan said. "Just high energy."

Jake shrugged.

Sabrina ran her fingers through her hair, making it look sex tousled. He stared at the bar, anything but looking at the sexy picture she made.

She spoke again, her voice much louder than usual. "I sure hope you can work things out with Olivia, Logan. I really, really do. Logan and Olivia. That's nice how your names are almost palindromes, L-o, O-l." No, they weren't, and she seemed a little too enthusiastic about the whole thing.

"Do you really, really hope that?" he asked dryly.

"Yes!" She poked his arm. "Ooh, call her right now and I'll tell her too."

"Sabrina, I think I should drive you home now."

"What! Why?"

"Because you're drunk."

She leaned close, smiling, her honey and flowers scent surrounding him, making him desperate to taste. "And you're in a relationship. I'm not! But nobody cares because I'm the relationship expert!"

Her brown eyes were glassy, but this was the closest she'd

ever been. A sharp tug of need had him leaning back. "Except you're not an expert, are you?" She'd said she'd had a committed relationship a long time ago. She was twenty-six, so he was willing to bet it was her one and only relationship. She hadn't been involved with anyone since. At least she'd never mentioned an ex.

"But I sound like one on TV!" she sang. "Claire has set me up good. All the hosts know her, all of them got the heads-up that we're friends, and all the questions will be so-o-o easy." She pounded the bar. "More Decadence, please!"

"Coming right up," Marcus said, pouring her another glass.

Logan stepped in. "Sabrina, you're going to get sick. How many glasses do you usually have?"

She slowly blinked at him. "I leave tomorrow for LA. Claire says you'll be in San Francisco by Thursday, so wave at me down there." She spread her hands a few inches apart. "We'll be this far apart according to Google Maps."

He couldn't help but laugh. She was an entertaining drunk. "Okay, I'll wave to you."

She held up a finger. "But stop waving on Sunday. That's when I go home."

"I go home the following Wednesday, so I'll wave to you on the East Coast." He spread his palms wide. "It's about this far apart on Google Maps."

She took a swallow of wine and frowned. "I'd better stop. Here, Marcus." She handed her glass back. "I don't want to be hungover on the plane."

Marcus took a sip from her glass, right where she'd sipped, his dark eyes glued to Sabrina.

Sabrina leaned across the bar and whispered loudly to Marcus, "That has my germs."

Logan slapped a palm on the bar. "He's flirting with you! God, Sabrina, don't you even know when someone's flirting with you?"

Her jaw dropped as she stared at him in shock.

Marcus shook his head at him. Alex and Ty got up and

left, Ty slapping a hand on his shoulder as he passed in some kind of brotherly solidarity.

Jake jerked his chin at him.

"What?" Logan barked.

Jake gave him a sympathetic look. "Might be time to check out another part of the party, bud."

Great. The heave-ho from his own brother.

"You know what?" Sabrina snapped. "I'll go. I don't need to sit here and get yelled at." She grabbed her phone, stood unsteadily, turned, and walked away.

She'd left her purse on the bench. He grabbed her purse, catching up with her as she moved unsteadily through the brick hallway toward the noise of the party. "Sabrina, I'm sorry."

She whirled. "It's a party! Excuse me for enjoying myself. And I can't help it if Marcus drank from my glass!"

He set her purse over her bare shoulder, his fingers grazing warm silky skin. "You're right. I'm just in a mood, I guess." And then he couldn't help himself, the words tumbling out. "You look stunning in that dress. It suits you."

She leaned close enough for his pulse to thrum, his body heating, primed for more. "It's Claire's," she said softly.

Do not touch her. She was drunk. He was not exactly single. They were *friends.* "It still looks amazing." His voice came out husky, his own lust betraying him. "Can I say that as your friend?"

She pursed her luscious pink lips like she had to think it over. "Sure, why not? Claire, Lexi, and Hailey said the exact same thing."

He was dying for a taste of her sweetness, nearly woozy with her scent—honey, flowers, and sweet Sabrina. "Guess I'm not very original," he murmured.

She sighed, her breath fanning his face. His gaze dropped to her mouth, the temptation of it made him lean in ever so slightly. Time stood still, the air crackling between them as they stood, nearly touching, sharing a breath. So close, so tempting, so *necessary.* The blood roared in his ears.

She took a step back and held up a palm.

He gave himself a mental shake. That palm was the stop sign on lust, but his lust wasn't going anywhere, still running full throttle through him, every instinct driving him to get closer. "Sabrina."

She blinked rapidly and took a deep breath. "I don't think we should be friends anymore. I can't…I just think we should say goodbye."

His chest clutched. "Why?"

"Because…" She let out a huge sigh. "Because you're leaving."

"Not right away."

She tilted her head. "And I kinda hate you a little bit for that when I should be happy for you, so goodbye."

They stared at each other. Was this really it? A drunken goodbye in his brother's basement? Her eyes watered, and she took in a shuddering breath like she was going to cry or something.

He offered his hand for at least a goodbye handshake.

She rushed at him, hugging him tight around the middle. No elbow squeeze, no awkward pat on the back, just a warm hug, her soft curves fitting perfectly against him. His arms went around her for only a moment before she pulled away.

Then she was gone.

And he was left standing there, suddenly cold and alone, wondering what the hell just happened.

8

Sabrina flew first class to LA courtesy of *The Joanne Show*, feeling extraordinarily tired. After she'd said goodbye to Logan, she'd been on the verge of tears and ran into Claire, who arranged for a ride home for her and then waited with her in the foyer while Sabrina babbled about how none of it had worked. Logan had noticed her dress, but he had absolutely no problem with all her good wishes for him and Olivia, and he'd even been cool with saying goodbye to their friendship. Never mind that the goodbye was what she'd wanted in light of his obvious devotion to Olivia. She'd held out a desperate hope that he'd step up, declaring Sabrina was too good a friend to let go. She sighed. It really was over. Logan was in the past.

Her future was ahead in a blooming career. She'd promised her literary agent she'd work up an outline for her relationship book while she was in LA, and she was excited by the idea. If only she could get past her total failure in the relationship department, then she could be open to whatever happiness awaited in the future. The hard thing was waiting for that future to happen.

She closed her eyes, her mind replaying the party last night for the hundredth time. She'd really tried to give Logan a signal, but she'd gotten more and more nervous about exactly how to do that without throwing herself at him, and ended up drinking more and more wine. He'd spent most of the time looking baffled, some of it entertained, and then he'd yelled at her just because Marcus drank from her glass. That was uncalled for. It wasn't like she'd done anything wrong. Although…he had said she looked amazing in Claire's dress. Of course, so did her friends, so that didn't mean more than a friend thing.

There was a moment there. A brief moment after he'd apologized when he'd leaned so close she'd thought they might kiss. And she'd wanted that more than anything, but then she'd remembered that was her attraction for him, not his for her. And he was with Olivia.

Goodbye, Logan. Hello, future happiness. She hoped. She deserved a little happiness, didn't she? She reclined her seat, tired of wallowing, and drifted to sleep.

She woke just before landing. Once at the airport, she found her ride, which whisked her off to a hotel in Beverly Hills. Her appearance on *The Joanne Show* was tomorrow afternoon. Claire had advised her to arrive a day early to get over the jet lag.

And what a day it was! She relaxed poolside, feeling decadent as she read *Married to my Fiancé* and sipped pomegranate-flavored iced tea. She could get used to this kind of life. Claire had arranged everything, and she couldn't thank her enough.

The next day she arrived at *The Joanne Show* for the one o'clock taping, refreshed and ready to go. The show would air at four o'clock today. She was whisked to hair and makeup, where first her makeup was applied and then her hair done. She wore her royal blue silk blouse with charcoal gray pants and her new metallic heels with wings. Claire had declared her outfit was the perfect middle ground between professional and stylish.

Joanne Fisher walked into the hair and makeup area to greet her. In person she was even prettier than on TV. She was probably in her forties, her dark hair highlighted with auburn, ending just past her jaw. Her eyes were brown, warm and sparkling with good humor. Like Logan's eyes. *Nope. Not going there.*

Joanne took the makeup chair next to Sabrina. "So you're the Hollywood Love Guru. Who's on your client list?"

Sabrina felt herself flush. Claire had encouraged her to embrace the label. It was, after all, the main reason Sabrina had been invited on all these talk shows. As uncomfortable as it was for her, knowing it had only been gossip that led to the label, Sabrina went along with it for the greater good. Her agent had assured her that the talk shows would lead to a lucrative book deal with a big marketing budget, which would mean a large audience for her book. That was what it all came down to for Sabrina—helping the most women she could with the kind of committed relationship they deserved.

Sabrina kept her tone professional. "Patient confidentiality means I never share identifying details."

"But you helped Claire Jordan."

Sabrina smiled, repeating herself. "Patient confidentiality means I never share details on any of my clients." Claire had advised her to repeat her answer over and over whenever she didn't want to go into more detail, until the interviewer moved on. It was better than saying "no comment," which Sabrina had thought sounded too closed off for a counselor.

Joanne shifted gears. "So I reviewed the tape from *Sunshine America.*" The makeup artist smoothed foundation on Joanne's face. "You mentioned helping your friends who struggled with committed relationships. Was that them having trouble committing or their boyfriends?"

Sabrina chose her words carefully. The last thing she wanted was to throw another friend under the bus. She didn't kid herself that anything said backstage wouldn't then be brought up in front of the cameras. "Eventually, there was a mutual commitment. My friends and I are in a singles book club, the Happy Endings Book Club, originally for the purpose of finding love."

"I love that! The Happy Endings Book Club!"

Sabrina smiled to herself, thinking of some of the early votes for club names. Mad had been campaigning hard for

SLUTS (Super Lovers of Underrated Terrific Stories). "It turned out no men were interested in dishing about books with us, so we dropped the singles part and just focused on the romance novels we all love."

"A romance book club. Cool! What's your favorite read?"

"We all loved the Fierce trilogy. That's how we met Claire Jordan. She was brought in by a former member, the author of the books."

Joanne grabbed Sabrina's arm. "Those books are so steamy."

"Right?"

Joanne looked up while makeup was applied to her eye. "So the Happy Endings Book Club is dedicated to romance, and you help your friends achieve that in real life. Is that how it works?"

"In a way, yes. We help each other, you know, bear witness to all the ups and downs. Everyone's so supportive."

Joanne pushed the makeup lady's hand back from her eye and leaned close to Sabrina. "I think I want to join this book club too."

Sabrina smiled. "We'd love to have you, but you'd have to move to Connecticut."

She laughed. "So have you worked things out with Logan?"

Sabrina tensed; the loss of him still fresh. But Joanne didn't know that. As far as everyone else knew, they'd had a lovers' quarrel on the street in Manhattan. "We'd like to keep our relationship private. Everything's fine, though." She was not about to declare a fake breakup of her fake relationship just before a big interview. Besides, she wanted to keep the focus on her career, not her crappy love life.

The makeup lady resumed adding eyeliner to Joanne's eyes, and Joanne got quiet. Good. Sabrina had handled that like a pro. She decided to ask a question of her own. "So—"

Joanne cut her off. "Were you and Logan really fighting like the article said?"

Sabrina worked hard to sound composed and professional. "No. We're more the talk-things-through type." At least that was what Claire had said they'd be like if they were actually a couple. Sabrina wasn't so sure.

Joanne pointed a manicured finger at her, saying in a singsong voice, "He looked pissed."

"That was taken out of context," Sabrina returned, unable to keep the sharp edge from her voice. "I'd like to avoid the topic of my relationship with Logan during our interview. Claire told me that was part of our agreement."

Joanne straightened. "I know my job." She tilted her chin as blush was applied to her face. "Just curious, you know, girlfriend to girlfriend."

"Gotcha. So tell me all about how you got *The Joanne Show.*"

Those were the magic words because Joanne went off on an animated description of her gradual climb to her own show, from bit parts on TV, to a brief stint as cohost of a morning talk show, to taking a break to be a mom, going in a completely different direction and doing standup comedy, appearing on other late night talk shows, and then finally landing her own show.

Sabrina relaxed, glad to have the focus off her and also really entertained. Things went smoothly from there. Joanne began their interview with a shout-out to the Happy Endings Book Club, and Sabrina said a quick hello to her friends through the camera. Just thinking of them made Sabrina feel supported. They'd watch this later and cheer her on.

Joanne kept true to her word, not mentioning Logan at all during their interview, not even asking about Sabrina's personal experiences at all. It was all about what Sabrina would recommend to people in different relationship situations, which was fun for Sabrina, tackling hypotheticals.

By the time the interview ended, Sabrina was elated.

"All clear," the director said, and the lights dimmed, the cameras turned off.

"I really enjoyed our interview, Sabrina," Joanne said warmly. "Thanks so much for choosing to appear on my show first." That had all been Claire's doing, being savvy to which shows Sabrina should do and in what order.

"My pleasure. I hope it was helpful to your viewers."

"I'm sure it will be."

She went backstage, gathered her things, and headed out the back exit, where her ride, another black Mercedes, waited. The moment she stepped outside, she froze, shocked by a crowd of paparazzi and reporters waiting for her. Holy shit! She was a relationship counselor, not a celebrity. Lights flashed in a flurry of pictures, momentarily blinding her. A microphone was shoved in her face. "Did you become a relationship counselor because you were left at the altar?"

Nausea roiled through her stomach, her skin cold and clammy.

More microphones appeared. "Are you going to Kevin's wedding?"

"Was your article a revenge piece against Kevin?"

"How does Logan feel about Kevin?"

"Do you help other jilted brides?"

Only her family and friends knew about Kevin. Oh, God, she was going to be sick.

The chauffeur, a large muscular man in his forties, shoved his way through the crowd and hustled her into the backseat of the car. The car door shut as more questions were hurled at her. Her friends wouldn't have betrayed her. She swallowed down bile and jabbed the lock on the door.

Someone pounded on her window, making her jump. The guy gestured for her to power the window down. She stared straight ahead, heart pounding, all of her nerves raw and jittery. A moment later, the car pulled away.

She rubbed her forehead. How did they know? And how was this going to bite her on the ass in her next interview? She grabbed her phone from her purse to call Claire. One of the publicists at Sabrina's literary agent's company had set up the interviews, but it was Claire who had personally contacted producers and smoothed the way. Only Claire had the pull to make demands on what topics were off-limits in Sabrina's interviews. Besides, she knew she couldn't count on her literary agent to run interference. When Sabrina had shared her concerns with Joyce about the psycho relationship counselor possibly sabotaging her, Joyce had cheerfully replied, "No such thing as bad publicity!"

The moment Claire answered, Sabrina told her everything, the story tumbling out in a rush of words.

"Sabrina," Claire said firmly, "I want you to take a breath, in and out. Stay calm. The last thing you want is to arrive at your hotel, find more reporters waiting for you, and blurt something in your emotional state."

"Okay," she managed in a strangled voice. She took a deep breath in and out.

"Now let's take this one thing at a time. I'll make some calls to the other talk shows to be sure that Kevin is not a topic for any interview. Give your agent the heads-up. If the producer doesn't sign off on it, tell your agent to pull the interview."

She ran shaky fingers through her hair. "Okay, okay."

"Now who knew about Kevin?"

"Everyone at the wedding, I guess. My family, his family, our friends from college."

"Are there still hard feelings between you and Kevin? Would he want to lash out at you?"

"No hard feelings on his part. He sent me an invitation to his wedding. He actually emailed too, wanting me to meet his fiancée."

"What a dick move!"

She calmed down a little with fierce Claire on her side. "I really don't see what he'd have to gain from telling people what he did though. It makes him look bad that he ditched me." She looked out the window, thinking hard. "Maybe if someone got in touch with my family. They love publicity and wouldn't hesitate to share. Though, so far, I haven't heard a peep from any of them. It's possible someone was digging into my past and found out Kevin and I applied for a marriage license that was never filed, or, I don't know, someone just started digging, talking to people who knew me back then."

"Who wants you to fall on your face?" Claire asked.

"Tara Brinkman. That relationship counselor I told you

about. She threatened me with a lawsuit, saying I was trying to steal her clients. I suspected she was the one behind that article on me and Logan supposedly having a lovers' spat."

"If she was motivated enough, I'd say it was her. The problem is proving it. We can't take legal action against her without some evidence."

"Legal action," Sabrina echoed, rubbing her temple.

"It's defamation of character, and you can sue her for it. You're a brand now, and we have to protect the brand."

She thought about that. She didn't know about the brand stuff, but damage to her reputation would definitely damage her career. "I don't even know where to start finding evidence. All I know is she's trademarked herself as the Commitment Counselor and had a *New York Times* bestselling book called *Goodbye Commitment-Phobe*."

"I remember her! Oh, yeah, she had her fifteen minutes of fame. She's probably just jealous of you."

"There is some overlap in our practices. She has an office not far from mine. One in Manhattan too."

"I'll get someone to dig into her a little more. See what she's up to."

She held the phone close, suddenly aware of the driver up front probably listening. "Claire," she whispered, "I'm afraid of what she might dig up."

"Are you somewhere private?"

"No."

"Call me when you are."

She let out a shaky breath. "Okay."

"Don't worry. You enjoy yourself out there, okay? It's not every day you're the toast of the town. Have some champagne and relax. I'm on it, and I've got your publicist's info too if I need it."

"Thanks, Claire. I'll call you later."

"Ciao."

She smiled at Claire's starry turn of phrase. "Ciao."

Welp. This was either going to be a glorious rise to a new stage in her career or a spectacular crash and burn. She'd find out soon enough. *Wait and see.* Augh. She was terrible about waiting. She wanted control of her life. She needed stability. This was exactly why she'd avoided the spotlight in the first place.

Sabrina's next interview wasn't until six o'clock the next day, so she had a good long while to fret. She'd called Claire back once she was back at the hotel and told her all about her nutso family, who never committed to anybody, and all her fears of being a fraud. Claire took it in stride, assuring her it wasn't anything they couldn't manage. The important thing, Claire said, was to stay on message, and that message was "Sabrina is a warm, professional relationship counselor that you'd be lucky to have on your side."

Sabrina had been reciting that motivational nugget to herself every time nerves got the better of her. She kept herself busy, working up an outline for her book and firing it off to her literary agent. Action was always better than inaction, especially in anxiety-filled times.

By the time she got to the studio for *The James Lyon Show*, a late night talk show, she almost wished Logan was there, standing in the background, supporting her in his quiet solid way. But Logan wasn't an option. They'd said their goodbyes. He was meeting up with Olivia Friday night after his most important investor meeting, and Sabrina wouldn't be at all surprised if he moved in with Olivia after that, cementing their relationship in San Francisco.

Her time at *The James Lyon Show* was conspicuously lacking in the warmth that Joanne had showed her. She'd been left to her own devices in a small dressing room with her name taped to the door, until just before filming when a crew member brought her to the very masculine set with a dark blue backdrop, a black desk, and light blue guest chairs.

Sabrina stood off camera, where she'd been told to wait for her cue. A studio audience was already in place, most of them young and male. Not exactly Sabrina's target demographic.

Claire had assured her this show was key to Sabrina cementing her status. When Sabrina argued she wasn't about status, Claire explained how that would translate into her book deal happening, which meant she'd reach a lot of people, men and women. Claire really understood Sabrina's priorities.

James Lyon finally appeared, striding on set, tapping his desk for some reason, and then heading toward the audience. He was in his thirties, his black hair slicked back, tall and lanky, with a ready smile. They weren't filming yet, the crew standing by for their cue. James waved to the studio audience before detouring to where she stood off camera, taking her hand in both of his and smiling. "So nice to meet you, Sabrina."

"You too. I'm happy to be here."

He gave her hand a squeeze before releasing it. "Your Happy Endings Book Club sounded interesting. Any other kind of happy endings going on there?" He winked and made an obscene gesture with his hand.

She didn't bother to keep the irritation from her voice. "No. And I don't like the way you're speaking to me."

"Touchy."

"I'm a professional, and I expect you to be too, on and off camera."

He adjusted his collar, pulling it away from his neck. "Yeesh, do I need to get my lawyer in on this?" His tone was jovial.

Sabrina was not amused. "Do I need to get mine?"

He grinned. "Feisty."

She stared at him.

"Come on, lighten up. Just having some fun with you. We're going to have a good show." He strode onto the set, taking his seat at the big desk.

She took a deep breath, hoping for the best, unsure what she was going to get from this guy. She didn't mind joking around, but she was a professional and wanted her work to be taken seriously. She was here to help people, not be the butt of a joke.

The show began. She waited for her cue before striding on stage, smiling at him before taking her seat.

"Sabrina Clarke, Hollywood Love Guru, everyone!" James gestured for the audience to applaud. They did, clapping and whistling. "Okay, okay." He gestured for them to quiet down and turned to her. "Great to see you here, Sabrina."

"Happy to be here."

"Any tips for a guy like me? How do I get a woman to commit?"

The audience roared with laughter.

She smiled good-naturedly. "Actually, both men and women can fear commitment. Sometimes it's an issue from their childhood that causes a lack of stability in their relationships." Her mind flashed to Logan, and his mom leaving his family. Her theory had been wrong in his case. He didn't have a problem with commitment. His brothers and sister were in committed relationships. His older brother, Josh, and his dad weren't. Commitment was a deliberate choice. But what made some people take that leap of faith and others not, given the same circumstances?

"Sabrina?" James waved a hand in front of her face. "Still with us?"

She blinked. "Sorry. Commitment comes with trust, something that builds gradually over time as two people get to know each other. It requires going beyond the surface to what's really meaningful to you."

James grinned. "I find a lot of meaning in beer."

The audience laughed.

Sabrina pasted on a smile, convinced Claire had agreed to the wrong show. Frat boy came to mind.

James got serious, saying with real sincerity, "I'd like to find love."

The audience quieted.

Maybe she'd been hasty in her judgment. Maybe he hid real vulnerability behind his jovial manner.

"Sabrina, you think a guy like me could find love through your romance book club?"

She took the question at face value, hoping he didn't make

any happy endings jokes because she just might smack him. "I think reading romance novels would be a great start. They celebrate everything important in life—love, happiness, working through whatever obstacles separate two people, and joining them together."

"Like the Fierce trilogy." He shook his fingers in the air and blew on them. "Hot."

She inclined her head. Everyone brought up the Fierce trilogy whenever romance came up, but those stories, based heavily on sexual dominance, were so much more than that. "I agree they're very hot stories, but they also have deeper themes of redemption and forgiveness. Romance novels have a lot to teach us, and I think more men should read them."

"I just might take you up on that." He looked to the audience. "Would you guys like to see me do that? Maybe we'll see how reading romance novels helps or hurts my chances with women."

The audience cheered and whistled. God, Sabrina hoped he didn't make those stories a point of ridicule. If he did, she'd have to start a campaign against him. She couldn't stand to have her advice twisted for a mean-spirited joke.

James laughed. "When we come back, we'll find out the qualities Sabrina looks for in a winning relationship."

Winning. Relationships weren't win or lose. They were give and take. She kept her mouth shut. She'd save that for the camera.

James turned and spoke to the director.

She sipped some water from the mug that seemed to be a staple for talk shows. This was going better than she'd expected considering his initial boorishness.

The show started again, and James fired off an unexpected question. "Sabrina, what qualifies you to be a relationship expert?"

She froze, all of her feelings of fraud coming to the surface before she ruthlessly pushed them down. "I'm a relationship counselor with a master's degree in psychology from NYU and a thriving practice of happy committed couples." She smiled. "At least they are when I get through with them."

The audience laughed. Not a huge laugh but still.

James rolled with it. "So what do you do to them? Make them give each other a bunch of lovey-dovey greeting cards?" He turned to the audience and stuck out his tongue. "Ugh, aren't they the worst?" His voice rose to a falsetto. "I love you forever and ever. I love you to the stars and back. Sickeningly sweet. What guy wants that?"

She jumped in as if he'd directed the question to her and spoke about the importance of good communication, starting with good listening on both partners' parts.

And he actually listened intently.

She sailed through the rest of the interview, feeling like she put some good stuff out there, and then she was done.

She left the studio, flying high. Some paparazzi and reporters waited outside, snapping pictures and calling out questions, but this time she was prepared. She didn't halt in her tracks, instead walking quickly to her car. The driver was already there, holding the door open for her. She was just about to get in when a harsh masculine voice asked, "Why is the Hollywood Love Guru single?"

She whirled to find that same photographer from New York with the long ponytail. "Who are you?"

"Logan Campbell was never your boyfriend. Why did you lie, Sabrina?"

A shiver went through her at his hostile tone. "No comment." This time she felt within her rights to shut down the question.

She got into the car and tried desperately for a deep breath. She couldn't get one, her chest muscles seizing tight with the effort. She breathed shallowly, dangerously close to losing it. It was hard to ignore the commotion of paparazzi outside as the car pulled away.

She wasn't sure if she was going to scream or cry, but the pressure inside her couldn't be contained. Not only did she hate being in the press for the wrong reasons, she hated Logan's name being dragged along with hers. She wiped away an errant tear. It was only a matter of time before her paparazzi dad showed up. He'd have no qualms about selling her out for a big payday. That was the sad and awful truth of her dad. He'd never cared about her and hadn't wanted to be a part of her life. She'd only met him for the first time at thirteen when he'd showed up to get some pictures of her mom with her art at the peak of her career. Hell, her mom would probably start reaching out to the press too, hoping to draw attention to her erotic paintings. *Fuck my life.* Could she not have just one good thing without all the complications?

She managed not to break down on the drive to the hotel. By the time she got back to the safety of her hotel room, she was thinking more clearly. She pulled out her phone, thinking of calling Claire again to see if she'd made any progress with building a case against Tara Brinkman, the woman Sabrina was beginning to think of as her nemesis. Her heart kicked hard at Logan's name on her phone screen. He'd texted her. They hadn't been in touch since Claire's party three days ago.

Logan: *I set up a Google alert on your name to see how you were doing out there. My name came up too. Call me.*

She stared at the text, the implications slowly sinking in. First, he'd cared enough to keep up with how she was doing, even after she'd told him goodbye. She warmed at the thought. Their bond was tighter than she'd realized. But if he saw his name linked with hers, he probably wasn't happy. He was trying to work things out with Olivia, and continued mention of Sabrina and Logan together wouldn't help that.

Before she called him, she set up a Google alert on her name. Everything in her seized, the pressure on her chest returning with a vengeance, and she broke out in a cold sweat. It was worse than she'd thought. The good articles describing her talk-show appearances and her article on commitment-phobes were completely eclipsed by the gossip. The picture of her and Logan fighting was everywhere. Numerous articles speculated on what the real story was between the two of them and questioned her qualifications. Even more articles speculated on which famous movie-star couples were on her client list.

Speculation on Hollywood couples didn't concern her, most of them pointed out happily married couples, but damage to her reputation from the other articles was a huge problem. All the articles questioning her qualifications quoted an anonymous source. If only she could find a way to prove it was that psycho Tara. She debated calling Tara and confronting her directly. Sabrina could assure her there were plenty of clients for both of them, no need for things to escalate. But what if their conversation made things worse? What if Tara used the conversation against her?

She called Logan.

"Hi," he said somberly. Despite the circumstances, the pressure on her chest eased just hearing his familiar deep voice.

"Hi. I'm sorry your name keeps getting linked to mine. It's awful. I don't know what to do. I can't prove who's behind it. Maybe it's just curiosity about me, but it feels malicious."

"It *is* malicious." He paused. "Look, I'm not sure what can be done, but this is screwing things up for me in more ways than one. It looks really bad for me to be getting all this press as some kind of, I don't even know, like a guy who doesn't have his head on straight, fighting in public, lying that we were together when we weren't. I let it go when you first mentioned us as a couple so you could save face, but I don't want to walk into those investor meetings and the first thing they think when they see me is that I'm a complete flake."

Shit. She hadn't even thought about that. First impressions mattered, and if they saw him through the salacious filter of gossip, it would be harder for him to be taken seriously. "I don't even know what to say. I feel terrible."

"Olivia's irate every time my name comes up on some crap website, even though it's the same story recycled over and over."

She wished Logan had let her talk to Olivia. She was sure she could've explained everything. "Are you still going to try to get through to her in person?"

"Yeah. We're supposed to have dinner Friday night after my meeting with Elias Gold. Big day for me."

That would be big. Logan had told her before that the meeting with Elias was the most important one. "Maybe you could try some kind of romantic gesture that shows how much you care, how dedicated you are." She was a masochist. Here she was, helping the man she wanted for herself. But she'd screwed things up for him, and, at least in relationship territory, she could be of some help.

"Yup. Flowers, jewelry, candy. I know the drill. You know what pisses me off though? Why should I have to apologize when I've done nothing wrong?"

"Don't look at it as apologizing." *It was more of a classic grovel.*

"But that's what it is."

"Think of it as an outward symbol of your love."

"That the kind of thing you tell your clients?" His skepticism came through loud and clear.

"Yes, what's wrong with it?"

"Nothing."

"What?"

"Just kind of hokey."

She huffed. It was bad enough she felt like a fraud, the gossips were stomping all over her reputation, and now Logan was questioning her abilities? "There is a love language that is meaningful to women. It's words, yes, but also actions. And I suspect you've been a little defensive, maybe letting some of your anger show with Olivia, when what she needs to hear is reassurance that she is who you want."

"If I've been pissed off, it's only because she's screaming at me."

"She's that mad?"

"That's what I've been telling you. Everything is fucked up. Please just get my name out of this mess."

"Okay, I'll do my best."

"Thanks. I caught your Joanne interview. You did great. You probably never needed me backstage."

The implication was clear. He'd been there for her and had been paying for it ever since. "I bet you wish you never showed up at *Sunshine America*. Then none of this would've happened."

"I don't do regrets. All right, I'd better get back to work. I'm flying out tomorrow, and I want to run through the presentation with Ben before I pack up the whole show."

She relaxed a little because now, despite everything, he sounded like the laid-back Logan she knew. He wasn't holding a grudge against her. He just wanted her to fix the fuckup. "Good luck!"

"Thanks."

She said a quick bye and disconnected. Then she looked up the Slater Foundation, figuring the least she could do was set the record straight with Olivia. She called her at work and left a message with her assistant.

Exhausted, she flopped on the hotel bed and threw her arm over her eyes. This would all be over soon, she reassured herself. Two more interviews tomorrow, one of them on an early morning radio show, and then a long weekend seeing some of the sights in California. She planned on renting a car and taking a drive south along the Pacific Coast Highway. This was supposed to be her vacation, after all, and she'd never been to California before. She planned to check out the beaches, the old Spanish missions, the seals in La Jolla, and spend a relaxing weekend in San Diego.

But it was hard to work up any excitement for sightseeing, knowing Logan was about to walk into the most important meeting of his life with all of this hanging over his head.

And the blame lay squarely on her shoulders.

9

———

Logan was so nervous for his meeting with Elias Gold he sweated through his dress shirt and had to change. This guy was the big kahuna, the one who could bring them to the next level. Not just because he had the big bucks. Elias had connections; he had clout. All of it would smooth the way for further growth, maybe even going public one day for the ultimate payday. That was how his brother, Jake, had become a billionaire. Logan mentally rehearsed his presentation on the drive over to Elias's San Francisco office. He had it down cold.

His mind drifted to Olivia. They'd be meeting for dinner tonight. He had a ruby ring for her and planned to pick up some roses. Ruby was her birthstone. He thought he should get big points for remembering it. It was the kind of gesture Sabrina would probably approve of. Things weren't going well for Sabrina. For some reason, there was continued attack coverage of her practice and personal life. The spotlight wasn't pretty. He understood better now why she hadn't wanted the attention in the first place.

He arrived in Elias's office, waited half an hour in the waiting room, where he nearly lost his cool, and was finally shown into Elias's huge corner office. Large picture windows gave a view of the city skyline and the bay beyond.

Elias didn't bother to stand, merely gesturing for Logan to

take a seat in one of the leather chairs across from his massive sleek black desk. Elias's chair was practically a throne, wide and tall.

Logan remained standing and reached across the desk to shake his hand. "Nice to see you again, Elias." They'd met once at a fundraiser in New York City, which was how he'd gotten this meeting.

"You too. Please have a seat."

Logan was six feet tall, but when he sat in the offered chair, he had to look up at Elias lounging on his throne. He suspected the guest chairs were lower than Elias's chair on purpose.

Elias folded his hands on his desk. "Logan, I agreed to this meeting, and I keep my word, but I must confess there's been some talk."

Logan wasn't about to offer any information on what that might be about. Could be Ben's false sexual harassment accusation, could be Logan in the press, or something worse he wasn't aware of. "What kind of talk?"

"You and a woman who bills herself as some kind of Hollywood Love Guru are all over the internet. Honestly, we don't need this kind of gossip. It does not inspire confidence to be the flavor of the day."

Logan took a deep breath. "Sabrina has been in the news a bit, but I assure you those reporters are just speculating. She's a friend of mine from home and is well respected for her work with couples. Must be a slow news cycle in January."

Elias grunted. "And I've also heard about Ben's sexual harassment charge."

"That charge was baseless. He was cleared of any wrongdoing."

Elias spread his palms wide. "Then why isn't he here today?"

Logan's gut churned. This was getting off to a bad start. "I agreed to take the lead on the meetings. He's holding down the fort back home. It's just a two-man operation."

"But you're the man behind software development. He's the finance guy."

"We share those roles."

Elias smiled, a cool smile that put Logan on the defensive. "So Ben does software too?"

He managed to sound calm. "No. But I do both."

Elias leaned back in his throne and crossed one ankle over his knee. "Seems inefficient."

Logan broke out in a sweat, belatedly wishing he'd insisted Ben come along. His business partner had felt strongly the black mark against him would hold them back. Logan had thought it might be better just to confront any concerns and deflect them, but Ben was still upset about the whole thing and didn't feel comfortable representing them in the meetings. "I can only do my job well when I understand where our financial priorities lie."

Elias put his leg down and leaned forward. "This shit makes shareholders nervous."

"Well, so far, we haven't opened up to shareholders."

"But you will one day. Isn't that the goal? Build your business, make bank, build another business. That's how most tech start-ups go."

He placed his palms on Elias's desk and leaned in. "Ben and I are dedicated to Checkin. This isn't a stepping-stone to something else. My goal is to bring in investment to build Checkin. We want a sales force, a marketing team, and an upgrade to our software to make it compatible with the dinosaur HR systems out there. Now can we talk numbers? Because I think you'll like the growth potential."

Elias slapped his desk. "Show me the numbers."

Logan breathed a sigh of relief and pulled out the report, handing it across the desk, and began to outline step by step how they'd started with checking employee backgrounds for other tech companies in the US and Canada, and slowly scaled up to other industries, but there were so many more they wanted to get into. He also had a video that demonstrated the software, but he'd save that for the team meeting if it got that far. Elias was all about the numbers. He'd already said he wouldn't bring his team into it unless he thought it was worth their time.

Twenty minutes later, it was Elias's turn to talk. He fired questions one after another, and Logan was able to answer most. And the one he couldn't, about branching out to Europe, he told him they'd think it over but had no immediate plans.

Elias scribbled on a piece of paper and slid it across the desk to Logan. "That's my offer."

Logan's eyes widened. Elias had offered double what they'd asked. Forty million dollars. He was momentarily speechless.

Elias spoke up. "I want a seat on the board and a vote in all business going forward."

Logan smiled big time, the tension draining from him. Not only did he have a generous offer in hand, the other investors might get excited and raise their offers even higher. "Thank you so much for this generous offer. I have a few more meetings set up. I'll get back to you no later than Wednesday."

Elias frowned. "You're taking this to other investors? Look, Logan, you know my reputation. My offer is on the table, and it expires close of business today."

Logan's stomach dropped. Shit. What was he supposed to do about those other meetings? Show up knowing he'd already made a decision? Cancel them before he even got a chance to hear what they might offer?

On the other hand, forty million dollars. Ben would tell him to go for it. Logan's instinct was to wait and see how things played out with the other investors, build some buzz, and go big.

Elias gazed at him steadily, his dark eyes gleaming. He definitely wanted in, which meant an enthusiastic partner.

Logan held out his hand. "Deal."

Elias gave it a firm shake. "Excellent. I'm glad to hear it."

"I'm available through Wednesday if you'd like to meet again with your team."

"Monday morning, nine a.m. sharp."

"Great." He stood. "See you then."

Elias picked up his phone and gave Logan a look like *what're you still doing here?* He was all business, no time for the social niceties like saying bye. What did Logan care? They'd gotten a very generous offer from a man who would be a great asset to them. It couldn't have gone any better.

He managed to wait until he was back on the sidewalk outside before letting out a whoop of victory, punching the air. He headed for his car, the brief moment of exultation fading to an urgent need to get started on everything he needed to do. He had to get Ben on the phone, cancel all the other investor meetings, and, oh shit, he still had to deal with Olivia.

Work first.

Sabrina finished her last interview late Thursday, which was the easiest of all. *The Chat* was exactly as it sounded, a cozy chat with four women hosts. She'd felt so comfortable it was almost like being with her own friends. The questions weren't even questions, more like statements about her great work and the importance of women standing up for what they wanted in a relationship. Of course, she couldn't have agreed more.

She headed out of the TV studio through a private back hallway, still a little stunned that she'd pulled off all the TV appearances this week. The radio show this morning had been short and sweet, no big deal at all. And tomorrow she'd start her real vacation. *Pacific Coast Highway, here I come!* She'd rented a Jeep for the vacation part of her trip, which seemed like it'd be fun to drive.

She ignored the paparazzi and reporters on her way out of the studio and calmly got into the waiting Mercedes. The shouted questions about her qualifications, her being left at the altar, and her relationship with Logan bounced right off her. This must be how celebrities felt. At first all the attention was disconcerting, and then it just became normal. She pulled out her phone to check her messages. Wow. Her office line had a ton of voicemail messages. She listened to the first one.

Hi, Sabrina, this is Patty Mercer. We're cancelling our appointment. No need to reschedule. Bye.

Strange. They'd been making real progress. She hadn't thought Patty and her husband were there yet.

Next message. *Hi, this is Warren Pitt. Take us off your calendar permanently.*

Okay, what was going on? She listened to the rest of the messages with building dread. Fifteen cancellations. What the hell? She went away for a week and lost half her clients?

She called Patty back, working hard to sound professional. "Hi, Patty, I got your message. I was wondering why you cancelled. Have you and Matt reconciled?"

"We're going in another direction," Patty replied tersely.

"You're breaking up? I actually thought we'd made some real progress—"

"We're going with the Commitment Counselor. We just really like her approach, and she's pretty well known. She wrote that book. I didn't go with her before because she was in the city, but she's expanding her hours at the Connecticut office, so we signed up. I'm sorry, Sabrina. We just like her reputation and think it will be a better fit."

"How did you hear about her?"

"I knew about her book before, but then I saw her advertisement everywhere—online, in my mailbox, on the local news channel. She sounds amazing and promises quick results. Plus the mailbox ad had a coupon for fifty percent off the first month's session!"

Sabrina hung up, nearly shaking with rage. She needed to calm down, get back to the hotel, and call all of her clients to assure them that she was the counselor for them.

It did not go well.

She sat at the desk in her hotel room, methodically going through every single cancellation with growing despair. They were not budging.

She dropped her head in her hands. All of the publicity had completely backfired. Instead of drumming up business and taking her career to the next level, it destroyed it. Bile rose in her throat and she rushed to the bathroom. She dry heaved into the sink, but nothing came out. She ran the cold water and splashed it on her face.

She stared at herself in the mirror. This was not the time to fall apart. This was the time to fight.

She went back to the desk, grabbed her phone, and called Claire, who brought her lawyer in on the call. The lawyer assured Sabrina he'd look into any wrongdoing and told her not to contact Tara until they knew what was what. Sabrina thanked him and hung up. And then she reached her limit, bursting into tears. Everything sucked, and there wasn't a damn thing she could do about it.

Eventually, she curled up in bed, watching mindless TV, done with reality.

The next morning, Friday, Sabrina was still on the jagged edge of her nerves. She was supposed to be enjoying a well-deserved relaxing weekend in San Diego, but she couldn't seem to work up even an ounce of enthusiasm for it. She felt helpless, unable to fix her client problem, unable to confront Tara, in waiting mode. She hated waiting. And Olivia, Logan's stupid jealous girlfriend, had never called her back either. Everywhere she looked was a complete fuckup.

She told herself it would all wait until Monday. She should just enjoy herself this weekend. She paced her hotel room. Maybe she'd skip the first-class ticket waiting for her on Sunday and buy a cheap flight home for today. Relaxation was not in her future. No, that was giving up. She'd regret not taking advantage of this rare opportunity to see the sights. She should take what little happiness she could.

She packed up her Jeep and got on the Pacific Coast Highway, telling herself she'd feel better once she arrived at her destination. A short while later, more and more agitated, she took the exit and made her way back on the highway in the opposite direction. There was only one problem she could tackle right away. *San Francisco, here I come!*

It was time to fix what she'd screwed up for Logan.

It was time for a little chat with Olivia.

10

———

Sabrina drove like a woman on a mission, stopping only once on the six-hour drive to San Francisco. She had it all planned out. She'd say she had to speak to Olivia about a large donation on behalf of Claire Jordan, yup, she went there, dropping her friend's famous name, and then she'd get into Olivia's office and have a calm rational talk. She'd tell her Logan had been her friend for quite some time and that she was also close with his sister, Mad. She'd tell her all the gossip surrounding Sabrina and Logan was just that and her lawyer was on it. She'd tell her to give Logan a second chance because he deserved it. He was a great guy.

Everything went very smoothly on the drive, which reassured Sabrina she was following the right path. She hit very little traffic, and she found a parking garage not far from the Slater Foundation.

Once in the building, she took the elevator to the fourth floor, went into the waiting area, and announced the purpose of her visit to the receptionist, a woman in her fifties with her black hair in a bob. The woman told her Olivia was in a meeting and she'd need to wait.

Sabrina took a seat, flipping through a magazine, hyper-aware of sounds from the nearby main office. Half an hour passed. It was four thirty. This seemed like the kind of job where people left at five, especially on a Friday.

Sabrina called over to the receptionist. "Could you please tell Olivia I need to see her? I can't stay much longer." Not true, she had nowhere to go, but she had to talk to Olivia *today*. Logan had said he was meeting Olivia for dinner tonight, and Sabrina wanted the problem to be fixed for him before then.

The receptionist checked her computer and looked up. "I'm sorry. Ms. Slater has the afternoon blocked off now. I could take a message, or we could arrange for something on Monday."

"I'm only in town until Sunday morning. I'll wait. Please let me know as soon as she's available."

She returned to her magazine, her only plan to catch Olivia on her way out, though she'd really prefer the privacy of Olivia's office for this conversation. She knew what Olivia looked like from the Slater Foundation website. She was beautiful with glossy long black hair, blue eyes, and flawless creamy skin. Just the kind of gorgeous woman Logan would want. As much as Sabrina wished it weren't true, her experience was that men were attracted first and foremost to looks. The biological underpinnings of the attraction for a fertile mate put aside, Sabrina thought it sucked. There were many wonderful intelligent loving women who would make excellent partners that were just passed by. Not that she was bitter. Much.

She pulled out her phone. No news from the lawyer or Claire, a few more voicemail messages on her office line. She was almost afraid to listen. If she lost more clients…nope, not going there. She'd wait to check on work after she finished here. One crisis at a time.

The receptionist left the front desk, grabbed a large plastic tag with a key, probably the key to the ladies' room out in the hallway, and left the office.

Sabrina shot out of her seat and dashed through the door to the main office. She slowed down a little, striding through like she belonged there, passing lots of offices along the periphery and rows of cubicles in the center. She figured Olivia, as the director, had the big corner office.

She could hardly believe it when she reached the corner office with Olivia's nameplate in gold outside it. Not a single person had batted an eye at her. The door was shut. Should she knock or just walk in? She glanced around at the busy staff. If she knocked, it might draw attention to the fact that she didn't belong. On the other hand, if she didn't knock, Olivia might be startled and loudly ask, "Who are you?"

She knocked softly. No answer.

Now or never. She quietly opened the door and shut it behind her, stepping into a large office with a modern light-toned wood and metal desk with a white leather executive chair, two white leather guest chairs, and, in the far corner, a round table with more chairs, but no Olivia. Hmm...maybe she was in a meeting room somewhere.

Sabrina took a seat in one of the chairs across from Olivia's desk. Eventually, she'd have to return here. No way Sabrina was walking into a crowded meeting room.

A bump and a soft laugh alerted her she was not alone. She looked around, spotting an adjacent door. Maybe Olivia had a private bathroom in her office. Nice perk.

The door sprang open. Olivia walked out laughing, her color high, her black hair mussed. She was busy tucking in her pink blouse, looking up at a man, a handsome Indian man, whose white shirt was completely unbuttoned. His belt hung open, the top button of his dress pants undone. Holy shit!

He buttoned his pants and did the belt. His eyes collided with Sabrina's. "Uh, we have company," the man said with a thick accent to Olivia.

Olivia finally noticed her and shrieked, "Who are you, and what're you doing in my office?"

Sabrina leapt out of her seat. "I'm Sabrina, Logan Campbell's friend. Who's that?"

"Logan sent you to barge in and spy on me?" Olivia barked.

Sabrina stared at the man. He buttoned his shirt as he

walked toward the door, where he stopped to put his dress shoes on. "Later, Livvie," he said and made a quick exit.

Sabrina turned back to Olivia, righteous indignation filling her. "Logan doesn't know I'm here. I came here today to ask you to forgive him, to tell you we really are just friends, and you shouldn't listen to the gossip, but now…I can hardly believe what I'm seeing here."

Olivia scowled. "You can't just barge into my office. I'm calling security." She rushed toward her desk.

"Wait! I just came here to help. I'll go."

"Hold on." Olivia studied Sabrina for a moment before wagging her finger. "I remember you now from all those gossip sites. The Hollywood Love Guru. Go find your own man."

Sabrina clenched her teeth. Should she tell Logan what she'd seen? It would break his heart. But she couldn't just let him move cross-country for a woman who didn't deserve him!

Olivia pulled a brush from her desk drawer and brushed out her hair. "I'm seeing Logan for dinner tonight, so you didn't need to come by after all. Goodbye."

"Do you want to be with Logan or with that man?" She gestured toward the door where the guy had just left.

Olivia rolled her eyes. "Not that it's any of your business, but Anil has an arranged marriage this summer, a merger of two very wealthy families. He's a friend."

How stupid did she think Sabrina was? They were obviously hooking up. And then it all made sense. "No wonder you were so jealous of Logan having a woman friend. Because *you* were guilty of cheating. People always harp on the thing they're most guilty of."

Olivia tossed her brush in the desk drawer, looking mildly irritated but otherwise too self-satisfied to care about Sabrina. "Look, I ended it with Anil. That was just our goodbye."

Oh, hell no! "Logan wanted to move out here for a committed future with you, and you're cheating on him all this time, leading him on?"

"I wasn't cheating. He's not here yet, is he?"

"But you have a long-distance relationship."

Olivia flopped down in her desk chair. "Whatever! I don't have to explain myself to you!"

Sabrina quickly put the pieces together. "You played him. You used Logan to put pressure on Anil, and it didn't work. Anil's still going through with his arranged marriage."

Olivia leapt from her seat. "Fuck Anil and fuck you!"

Sabrina whirled and rushed for the door. This was all kinds of wrong. Logan deserved so much better than this manipulative bitch. She'd just reached the door when Olivia threw out her last jab.

"If you tell Logan about Anil, I'll deny it. It'll be my word against yours!"

Sabrina turned, opening her mouth to inform her she most certainly would be telling Logan, when Olivia went on in a much calmer voice.

"Logan proposed to me in college. Circumstances weren't right then; now they are. So be a good friend to him and keep your mouth shut."

Sabrina suppressed her shock. He'd proposed? But he'd told Sabrina it was hard for him to imagine committing to forever when the odds were stacked against it working out. Was Olivia the reason he felt that way? Did Olivia want to marry Logan to rub it in Anil's face?

Olivia spoke up. "You can go now."

Sabrina just stood there, taking in this beautiful woman who was a manipulative cheating liar. A terrible partner for Logan.

Olivia picked up the phone on her desk. "I'm calling security."

Sabrina left without another word.

She stepped outside, thought about calling Logan and telling him everything she'd just witnessed, and then quickly decided she needed to tell him in person. It was a delicate situation that had to be handled with great care. Logan was staying at Claire's house, so she texted Claire for the address. Definitely better for Sabrina to just show up than to tell him they needed to talk and have him worry until she reached him. All she had to do was get to him before he left for dinner with Olivia.

A few minutes later, she was on her way with Claire's blessing. "Go get him!"

~

Logan drove north to Claire's beachfront home, a surprisingly modest four-bedroom Cape Cod-style home worth millions purely for its location. He'd taken Claire up on her offer to stay there mostly because she'd asked him to look in on it and make sure everything was in order. She had a caretaker, who stopped by twice a month, but she wanted him to give her the real scoop. He suspected she just wanted to take care of him. Ever since she'd married his brother Jake, she fussed over the rest of them. When he'd arrived yesterday, he'd discovered the caretaker had fully stocked the refrigerator for him, laid fresh towels out, and made up every single bedroom with supersoft gazillion-thread-count sheets. He'd taken the king-size bed in the master bedroom when he'd arrived last night and couldn't deny he relaxed more at Claire's house than he would have at a hotel.

He pressed the code for the metal gate and pulled into the driveway. The security here wasn't as tight as he'd thought it would be. There was a waist-high brick wall around the street side of the property with the metal gate, but a determined Claire Jordan fan could easily scale it or approach from the private beach and climb up the back deck. Of course, there were security cameras, and Claire normally stayed there with her bodyguard in the nearby guest cottage on the property.

He let himself in the front door with the security code, stepping into the bright open-plan first floor. The great room with high ceilings, white walls, and light hardwood floors was the main living space, with the kitchen just beyond it. Colorful geometric area rugs defined two sitting areas and a dining area. The beige sofas and chairs held bright colored throw pillows. It was all very cozy, not sleek and glam like he'd expected.

He made his way through the great room to the gourmet kitchen with its stainless steel appliances, white cabinets, and light tan granite countertops and set his jacket and tie over the back of one of the wrought-iron swivel stools at the center island, leaving his laptop on the island counter. He snagged a bottled water from the refrigerator and took a long drink. He'd filled Ben in on Elias's generous offer and stipulations on the drive up. Ben had been thrilled, of course, exclaiming loudly for several minutes about the amazing news.

Now there was nothing to do but celebrate. Claire had left a bottle of champagne in the fridge with a note that said *For your celebration.* Such a sweetheart, her faith in them absolute.

He leaned against the counter. All that buildup, all the worry and stress and preparation, and here it was—success. This was what success felt like. Exhilarating, satisfying, but oddly quiet.

He wished Ben were here to celebrate with. He supposed he could have champagne with Olivia later, but for some reason, he didn't want to celebrate this with her. She didn't know all the work that had gone into this moment. Sabrina knew all the nitty-gritty, had listened to him go on and on about it, but she was down in LA. Maybe he could text her the good news. She'd told him goodbye, but a text wasn't too personal, and they had been in touch when his name got linked with hers again in the gossip rags.

He pulled out his phone just as a chime went off in the house like a muted doorbell. He stuck his phone back in his pocket and headed over to the front door. Maybe it was the caretaker checking in to see if Logan needed anything. He checked the monitor screen by the door that showed the outside view. No one was there.

He stepped outside and saw a red Jeep by the gate. He walked a little closer, and the driver's side window powered down. Sabrina poked her head out with a wave. "Hi, it's me! Can you let me through?"

He stared at her in shock. "Sabrina! I thought you were in LA!"

She gestured to the gate. He nodded, went back inside,

and pressed the button. Claire had given him instructions on letting a visitor in, just in case he wanted to have Olivia over. But it was Sabrina. He still couldn't believe she was actually here. Now he didn't have to celebrate alone. She parked in the driveway behind his rented black BMW.

He held open the front door. "Come in! What're you doing here?"

She wore one of her professional outfits—red lacey short-sleeved top with white dress pants and beige flats. He was still in his business-meeting clothes, a white button-down shirt, gray suit pants, and black leather shoes. He'd figured he'd need the outfit for the fancy restaurant tonight with Olivia.

Strangely, Sabrina didn't smile at him like she normally would. She walked at a brisk pace and stepped inside, her expression serious. "Claire told me you were staying here. I wanted to stop by."

"You okay?" he asked. "How was the drive?"

"I'm good." Her tone brightened. "Drive was good."

"I was just about to have a celebratory glass of champagne. We got an incredible offer from Elias. Done deal."

She beamed, and it was like the sun came out. "Oh, Logan! That's wonderful! I'm so happy for you and Ben!"

He smiled back, thrilled to share this with her. "Thanks. Want some champagne?"

She got serious. "Maybe we should talk first."

His brows drew together in concern. "Did something happen? Is that woman harassing you some more? What a bitch." Sabrina had been through the wringer with all the media attention.

She bit her lip. "How much time do you have before you meet Olivia for dinner?"

He glanced at his phone. "About an hour." He studied her. "What is it?"

She went to the overstuffed white sofa and patted the seat next to her.

He took a seat and looked at her expectantly. "Well?"

She took a deep breath and folded her hands in her lap.

When she spoke, it was in her reserved professional counselor tone. "I have a theory that people become most upset about what they themselves are guilty of."

"O-kay," he said slowly, not sure where she was going with this. He hadn't done anything to feel guilty about.

"Shit." She pressed her fingers to her forehead and closed her eyes.

"What?"

She met his eyes. "I just realized how that applies to me. I have a thing against commitment-phobes—" her palm rested against her heart "—and I'm a commitment-phobe. That's why I haven't had a relationship in years. Ugh. The irony. I'm the person I warn people about."

He cocked his head. "What? No way. You dedicate your life to helping couples commit to each other. That's your thing."

She sighed. "That's my thing for others, yes. But, for me, I haven't had a committed relationship since my ex left me at the altar." She paused, and when she spoke again, her voice was real and raw. "Logan, it was so humiliating, me standing up there in my wedding gown, all of our family and friends there, and then he just walked out the back door of the church and never looked back."

"Bastard," he spat. He wanted to punch the guy.

She gave him a tight smile. "Thanks." She hesitated before saying, "I think it affected me more than I realized. I longed for a relationship, yet did nothing to find a meaningful connection that might one day lead to that."

His brows scrunched together in confusion. "So you drove all the way up from LA to confess that you're a commitment-phobe? Don't feel bad. Obviously you know what you're doing with other people. Now you can just apply the same advice to yourself."

She stared straight ahead. "I stopped by the Slater Foundation."

An uneasy feeling went through him. Olivia would tear sweet Sabrina to shreds. "You did?"

She faced him. "I wanted to fix what I'd screwed up for

you. I just wanted to assure Olivia she had nothing to worry about where you and I were concerned."

He grimaced. "I'm guessing it didn't go well."

"No. It went very, very badly." She spoke slowly as if trying to ease into treacherous territory. "I guess what I'm trying to say is…my theory that people become most upset about what they're guilty of…" She paused, searching his expression, before finally saying, "Well, that might apply to Olivia too with her jealousy issues."

He read between the lines. "You mean her jealousy and accusations are because she's guilty of cheating on me?"

"Yes," she said softly. Her eyes were big and sympathetic. "I went to her office, and she was with a man in her private bathroom. They came out half undressed, obviously having hooked up. She as much as admitted—"

"That's enough." He stood and walked a few steps away. Could this be right? Olivia was cheating on him after all the fuss she'd made over him having relationships, even friendly ones, with other women? Olivia was the one who had reached out to him. Why would she do that if she was already in a relationship?

Sabrina spoke up. "There's more you should know."

He shook his head. "I'll call her, figure out what's what, and then you can have some champagne with me. Help yourself to the fridge if you're hungry."

He was heading for the stairs to call Olivia in privacy when Sabrina called out urgently, "She was using you to put pressure on her boyfriend, Anil, not to go through with his arranged marriage, but he's still going through with it. I'm not sure if you were her plan B, or she hoped to marry you to rub it in his face. Maybe both."

He closed his eyes for a moment. Here he'd been thinking they had something real when he'd been played. If what Sabrina said was true. He needed to talk to Olivia and hear it directly from her. He held up a hand in acknowledgment to Sabrina and continued upstairs to the master bedroom, closed the door for privacy, and called Olivia.

"Hello," she purred. "Can't wait to see you tonight. It's been so long."

"Olivia, Sabrina told me everything. You're with Anil, using me to force his hand and make him not go through with an arranged marriage. He's still going to marry this other person. Please tell me if this is true."

"I ended it, I swear. I was a fool to be with him. You're my future."

He pinched the bridge of his nose. Dammit. He couldn't believe he'd let it get this far with her. He'd been ready to leave his family and friends behind and move cross-country to solidify their relationship when there was no relationship. He'd let their past connection in college weigh too heavily on their future.

"Logan, please, you and I never explicitly said we were exclusive."

"Then why the hell were you freaking out that I might be with Sabrina!" He exhaled sharply. "This is over. Goodbye, Olivia." He disconnected, beyond aggravated. Then he deleted Olivia's contact info from his phone. A small vengeance.

He stood there for a minute, letting himself cool down before heading downstairs. He found Sabrina in the kitchen, washing some green grapes. He waited for her to turn the water off before saying, "Hey."

She whirled. "Are you okay?"

"Yeah." He lifted his palms. "I ended it with her."

She set the grapes on some paper towels and dried her hands. "I'm so sorry. I know you were hoping things would go very differently."

He pressed his lips together, still pissed he'd been so fooled by Olivia. "Yeah, well."

Sabrina spoke in a gentle, soothing tone. "I just couldn't let you move forward not knowing what she was about."

He nodded. "Thanks, you saved me from a huge mistake. Want to get drunk?"

11

____

"Let's do it," Sabrina said and immediately blushed.

Logan studied her. Wait, was she blushing because that sounded dirty? Was she into him?

She fluttered a hand in the air. "I mean, I've had a really shitty week. I actually considered flying home early, tail between my legs."

He knew her week had been filled with malicious gossip. Obviously, it was his own dirty mind turning her words into something more.

He crossed to her and made a show of looking behind her. "Never noticed a tail on you."

She laughed. "You're taking this much better than I thought. I was so afraid you'd be devastated."

He studied her for a moment, all concern for him. She really cared. "You're a good friend."

She looked away, blushing. "I try."

He got the champagne from the refrigerator and opened it, the pop echoing satisfyingly in the large open space. The start of a celebration. Sabrina set two champagne flutes on the counter that she'd found in the cabinet. He filled them and lifted his glass in the air. "To Elias!"

She lifted her glass. "To Checkin and all of your and Ben's hard work."

They clinked glasses and drank. Damn, this was some good champagne. Leave it to Claire to spring for the good stuff.

He lifted his glass to hers again. "To good friends."

She smiled, a warm tender smile that reached in and squeezed his heart. He was so lucky to have her on his side. "To *great* friends."

They drank to that.

Sabrina set her glass on the granite counter behind her and hopped up on the counter, taking a seat. "Tell me all about your meeting today. I want to hear every detail."

He sat on the island counter across from her and told her everything, right down to sweating through his first dress shirt.

She slapped the counter. "I love it. I knew you'd kick ass."

One corner of his mouth lifted. She rarely cursed. Must be the champagne. She'd finished her glass while he was talking. He refilled her glass, finished off his, and refilled his glass too.

He clinked glasses with her. "To kicking ass."

"I'll drink to that!" She drank, wiped her mouth with the back of her hand, and gave him a big beaming smile that grabbed him by the balls. Sabrina flushed pink, relaxed and happy was a sight. A vision of a sated Sabrina in bed, her long dark blond hair spread out on the pillow, relaxed and smiling at him, flashed through his mind. She shook her shoulders out. "Woo! I'm starting to feel the champagne."

"Yeah? Good." His voice came out husky. Geez, he wasn't going to move in on his friend just because he was now a free man.

He was a free man.

Sabrina was single.

Nope. She wasn't giving him a signal. She was just a little tipsy.

Some lines you couldn't uncross.

He returned to his safe perch on the island across from her. "Your turn. Tell me all about your talk-show run. I already know the gossip shit, and that, by the way, is no concern of yours."

She scowled. "I'm so pissed! Half my clients cancelled on me. Tara is running all these local ads, stealing them away. She wants to ruin me."

"Holy shit. Half? But you got a lawyer on it, right? And I'm sure Claire's all over it."

She stared at the floor, her shoulders drooping. "Yeah, but it still sucks."

His chest ached in sympathy. He left his glass on the counter, closed the distance between them, and tipped her chin up. "We're not going to let that ruin our celebration. I kicked ass today. You kicked ass all week. You might've lost some clients, but you'll get more. Tenfold."

Her brows shot up, her eyes big and hopeful. "You really think so?"

"I know so. Time for some celebration music." He pulled out his phone and cued up his workout music, blasting it. Mostly fun pop songs with a good beat like "Pump It" by the Black-Eyed Peas.

She laughed. "What is this?"

He grinned. "It's music to get me through my morning workout."

She hopped off the counter and started dancing, hands in the air, rocking out. He joined her, grabbing her hand and spinning her around. She laughed and he spun her back. She lost her balance and slammed into his chest, giving him a jolt of awareness, soft curves pressed against him. His hands went to her bare arms, warm and satiny soft.

"Sorry," she said, patting his chest and backing away.

The music kept blasting, but all of his focus was on Sabrina scooting back onto the counter, sipping champagne, her brown eyes bright, her cheeks flushed. He wanted to feel her pressed against him again. The intense need to get closer blocked out the reasons he had to keep his distance. He finished his champagne, watching her, his mind fuzzy, his body warm. Then he turned down the music and joined her.

He sat on the counter next to her, leaving no space between them, his thigh right up against hers, his arm brushing hers. She stayed put, her cheeks flushing bright pink. It must be him that made her blush, not shyness, which meant…she wanted him. He breathed in her sweet scent, honey and flowers and sexy woman. He didn't have to pretend he didn't notice anymore. When she wasn't in her cool professional mode, she was an incredibly sexy woman, warm, open, and soft.

He lowered his voice to a deep husky tone. "I missed you this week."

Her head shot up, meeting his eyes with a look of surprise. Her voice was whisper soft. "I missed you too."

He smiled. "You know, there's no reason for me to move to San Francisco now. Ben and I can handle most stuff online, with a few business trips to nail down the details. Looks like you're stuck with me in Connecticut. What do you think about that?"

She smiled back. "I'm happy to hear it."

"So you don't need to tell me goodbye." He nudged her shoulder. "You can tell me hello again."

She laughed. "Hello."

He gazed into her eyes. "Hello."

She sighed. "I'm so relaxed now." She hopped off the counter and pointed at him. "I'm going to make you dinner. You're welcome."

"You don't have to do that. We could go out somewhere."

She made her way to the fridge. "I like to cook, and you've got so much food." She opened the refrigerator door and started pulling stuff out. "You can make the salad. And, let's see, I'll make…" More and more food appeared on the counter as Sabrina dug in. Then she found a pantry and flung the door wide. She turned to him. "I'll make lemon chicken, roast potatoes, and carrots."

"Sounds great."

She beamed. "Awesome. Look around for a big salad bowl and a colander. Oh, and after the salad's ready, can you set the table?"

"Sure thing."

She did a little hip wiggle. "Turn the dorky music back up too."

"Dorky!"

She laughed. "I like music when I cook."

"What do you listen to?"

"I'm a big Adele fan."

"I only have *real* rock music on my phone."

She waved airily. "Whatever."

He scrolled through his playlists, looking for something to set the mood. He didn't have any romantic songs. He wasn't all that sentimental, but...Sabrina. She was going out of her way to cook him dinner. She was relaxed from the champagne, and the moment was ripe for making a move.

He texted Claire. *Sabrina's here cooking dinner. You have some kind of built-in sound system?*

Claire: *Yes! The control is over in the sitting area in the white cabinet. Good luck!*

He stared at his phone and quickly texted back. *Good luck?*

Claire: *Ciao!*

Did Claire want him to be with Sabrina? He hadn't even told her he'd ended it with Olivia. Or had Sabrina confided in Claire that she was into him?

He glanced over at Sabrina, who was pounding the shit out of the chicken breast with a meat tenderizer.

She looked over at him, smiling. "This is very therapeutic!"

"If you say so." He headed over to the sitting area in search of the music control.

"Salad is over here!" she caroled.

"I'm getting your music going. Claire told me it's in here."

"Okeydokey."

He chuckled to himself. She was so cute when she was tipsy. A few minutes later, he got the music going. Slow jazz. *Aw, yeah.* Mood music.

He returned to the kitchen, and Sabrina pointed to a colander on the counter. "Rinse, dry, and rip the lettuce into bite-size pieces."

"Bossy."

She used the side of her arm to push a lock of hair out of

her face, her hands covered in flour, which she was dredging the chicken in. "Chef rules the kitchen, minion."

He closed the distance between them and smoothed the errant lock of hair behind her ear before leaning down to whisper, "I get that. I like to be in charge sometimes too."

Her head whipped toward his, her eyes wide. "Are you referring to a, um, different room in the house?" Her voice got high and squeaky at the end there.

He leaned against the counter next to her. "Have you ever thought about you and me?"

She turned from him, staring at the chicken, her cheeks flushed pink. "Have you?"

"I'm starting to."

"Oh."

"Well?"

She met his eyes. "I'm not exactly starting to."

He straightened. "Got it." Good thing he checked in before crossing that line. That could've really backfired on him, tanking their friendship, making everything awkward as hell. He went to the sink and got to work on the salad.

Sabrina wasn't moving, just standing there, staring at the chicken.

"That chicken's not going to cook itself," he teased.

She shook her head. "I spaced out. Lo-o-o-ng day. Back to work."

They worked in silence, the music relaxing, the champagne having done its part. He caught her watching him several times, probably because he kept sneaking peeks at her. A few times she opened her mouth and then shut it again. Probably trying not to boss him so much since he'd teased her about it. Friends was not the worst thing in the world. It wasn't like he was desperate or anything. Maybe once the champagne wore off, she'd go back to her untouchable porcelain-doll self and he wouldn't even be tempted.

~

An hour later, Sabrina served up dinner and carried two plates to the dining area, where Logan was already seated at the round wooden table. She was kicking herself for her completely unflirty response to Logan's question. *Have you ever thought about you and me?* Why hadn't she just said the truth? Yes! Way too much! Her response, while honest, hadn't moved things forward. She wasn't *just starting* to think about the two of them, she'd been thinking about them since the first time he'd stepped foot in her office six and a half lust-filled months ago, leaned one muscular arm against the door frame, smiled his gorgeous smile, and told her they'd be neighbors.

Why couldn't she be flirty? It was like she had no game. Sadly, the champagne had worn off, and now she was facing another friendly meal with Logan, wishing she could somehow steer the conversation back to the two of them and —fuck it. She was going to have some wine. She just had to stop overthinking everything. She was here. He was here. Both of them single. If it didn't happen tonight, it wasn't ever going to happen.

"Sabrina, this all looks fantastic," Logan said, staring at his plate.

"Thanks. You want some wine?"

"Sure, if you're having some."

"Oh, yeah." She headed toward the kitchen, where she'd spotted a small wine refrigerator.

"Oh my God," Logan said loudly from the dining area.

She froze. "What's wrong?"

"This is amazing! I didn't know you could cook like this! It's better than a restaurant."

She beamed. "Glad you like it."

He took another forkful of chicken. "I love it."

She smiled to herself and continued on to the wine refrigerator. At least she'd done that right. A few minutes later, she returned to the table with an opened bottle of some very expensive sauvignon blanc and two wineglasses. She poured some for both of them and took her seat.

"Claire has really good taste in wine," she told him.

He kept eating, ignoring his wine. "Money'll do that for you."

She sipped the wine, savoring it for a moment, and then she chugged. So sue her. She had a lot riding on this. She cut into her chicken and took a bite.

Logan was really into his food and didn't even look up when he said, "You leave on Sunday, right?"

"Yup. Sunday morning."

"You can stay here if you want. There's plenty of room. Four bedrooms upstairs." He glanced up at her. "Unless you have other plans."

My plan is to seduce you. "I'd planned a solo trip down to San Diego, but…I'm flexible." She tossed back her wine while he devoured his meal. "So if I stayed here, what would we do?"

His head jerked up. "Whatever you want."

She traced a circle on the table with her index finger, trying to figure out the best way to suggest they return to that whole you-and-me thing.

Logan took a sip of wine. "This *is* good wine. If you've never been to San Francisco, I could show you around. I went to college out here."

"Mmm, maybe," she said noncommittally.

"Or we could just hang out. Watch a movie or something."

She studied him. He gave her a quick smile and went back to eating. He wasn't giving out a flirty vibe at all. It was like he'd shut the whole thing down and was firmly back in friend territory. She'd appreciate his respectful boundary if she wasn't so mad at herself for blowing her chance.

"Aren't you going to eat?" he asked. "It's so good."

"Sorry. I guess I'm more tired than I thought. I keep spacing out." She went back to eating.

Logan refilled her wineglass for her and grinned. "I gotta admit I find a tipsy Sabrina very entertaining."

"Why? Do I say stupid things?"

"No."

"Well, do tell, what do you like about a tipsy Sabrina?"

She leaned across the table, smiling at him. See, she could be flirty.

He chewed and swallowed. "You're much warmer. Usually you're like an untouchable porcelain doll."

Stung, she leaned back, her stomach souring. "Oh." *Untouchable.* Maybe that was why she hadn't been with a man in so long. She gave off an untouchable vibe. The label *hurt.* Probably because the one man she really wanted to touch her had said it. That whole flirty thing earlier had been because they were both tipsy. Now Logan was stone-cold sober and thought she was…untouchable.

"Sabrina, I didn't mean to hurt your feelings."

She shook her head, staring at her plate, telling herself just to move past it. So he thought she was untouchable. Big picture? No. There was no bigger picture where she could see any sunnier side to this. It just sucked.

"Hey," he said gently, "maybe I just don't know you well enough. I mostly see you at the office."

She clenched her jaw. You know what? She was very touchable. She had a lot going for her—a loving, empathetic nature, good friends, a career that helped a lot of people. At the thought of her career and losing half her clients, she totally lost her cool. Enough already!

She took a big swallow of wine and jabbed a finger at him. "Here's what I think about you."

He pounded his chest with one fist. "Let me have it."

"Never mind," she said quietly, looking away. She shouldn't take out her frustration on him. "It's uncharitable."

He laughed. "Great! Insult me so I can stop feeling like a jerk for calling you a porcelain doll, which can be quite pretty, by the way. Not that I ever had one." He lifted a finger. "But I have seen them."

"Yes, but porcelain has negative connotations when applied to me." She exhaled sharply. "You really want to know?"

He spread his arms wide. "I really want to know."

She crossed her arms. "I thought you were a commitment-phobe."

"Oh, boy. Number one on your shit list."

She inclined her head. "But then I found out about Olivia."

He speared a carrot. "So I guess we both misjudged each other."

"I guess." She sighed, ate a little more, and finished her wine. She had just enough of a buzz to drown out her earlier regret. It wasn't too late. She just had to make one move, one lusty signal, to prove to him she wasn't an untouchable porcelain doll. She was sure he'd take it from there. Hadn't he implied he liked to be the boss in the bedroom? That had to be what he meant about being in charge sometimes. Otherwise, why would he have whispered it in a husky voice that sent shivers through her? She really hoped that was what he meant because it would be *so* much easier for her. She wouldn't get worked up so much, wondering how she was doing. She'd only been with her ex. None of her other dates since then had progressed past the second date. Sure, she'd kissed a bunch of guys, got felt up, but as to the actual deed, not so much. That was on her. She'd been afraid to have a real meaningful connection. Now she was ready. And she trusted Logan.

She watched him finish his dinner and wipe his mouth with a napkin. He'd cleaned his plate.

He looked up at her and flashed a smile that made her heart kerthunk. "Amazing. Compliments to the chef. I'll wash the dishes since you cooked. And by wash, I mean I'll put them in the dishwasher." He winked.

She laughed. "Fair enough."

He stood and took both their plates. "You spending the night?"

Now or never. "Yes."

"Awesome. Go ahead and make yourself comfortable upstairs. All the bedrooms are ready for guests."

"Okay, thanks."

"Thank Claire," he said and headed to the kitchen.

"Thanks, Claire!" she sang to the ceiling.

He stared at her. "Are you tipsy again?"

"A little," she admitted. "I'm trying to lose my untouch-able porcelain-doll image."

He gave her a sympathetic look. "I shouldn't have said that."

She shook her head. "Don't worry about it. I'm going to get my suitcase."

She returned with it a few minutes later, went upstairs, and scoped out the bedrooms until she found the one with his suitcase. She went right on in. Maybe her suitcase would do the talking for her. Ha-ha. She pulled out her phone and cancelled her hotel reservation. There. No going back. Next step, seduction readiness. She dug her toiletry bag out of her suitcase, went to the en suite bathroom, and freshened up.

Deep breath and go!

She went downstairs and took a seat at the island, watching him clean up. Nothing sexier than a man cleaning up the kitchen. Seriously, this could be porn for women. *Boom-chicka-wow-wow.* Watching his broad back in a white dress shirt, tapering to a trim waist and very nice ass show-cased beautifully in suit pants, as he loaded the dishwasher made her want to rip his clothes off.

He finished up and turned to her, hands on his hips. "You tired?"

Tired? No. Determined? Yes. "I'm not a doll, Logan, and I'm not delicate. I won't break."

He rubbed his light brown beard. "I get that now."

She shared some more, making sure he got that image out of his head for good. "I grew up in a Manhattan loft surrounded by erotic paintings of couples and threesomes." She lifted her palms. "That was my childhood. So if I seem, I don't know, reserved, it was only my act of rebellion against my embarrassing mother."

He crossed to the island, leaning one hand on the back of her chair, looking down at her and grinning. "Learn anything?"

She shuddered. "More than I ever wanted to know."

"So-o-o," he drawled, "ever try that stuff?" A smile played over his lips, his brown eyes dancing with amusement. God, he smelled good. He always smelled fresh and clean, but today he had on some kind of woodsy cologne that made her want to lick him from head to toe.

"The point is…" She had a point, didn't she? Her mind was fuzzy with his proximity and too much wine. "I am not my mother. Thank God!"

"Amen," he returned. "Not that I know your mother. She might be a very nice woman. So were the threesomes two women and a guy, or two guys and a woman?"

She narrowed her eyes. "Does it matter?"

"Uh, yeah," he said, like *duh*.

"It was two guys and a woman. I think it was her fantasy."

"Or her reality."

Sabrina held up a palm. "Moving on! Here's what else I used to think about you." Almost there. She was building her case.

"Hit me. I'm loving an unfiltered Sabrina."

"I thought you were a risk taker."

"It's not like I jump out of airplanes. Ty's the risk taker in our family." His brother, Ty, used to be a stuntman.

"I realized I was wrong about the risk-taking," she said with a smile, hoping it was clear that she wanted him even more now that she knew him better. "You're actually quite stable and nicely risk-averse."

His brows scrunched together like he wasn't following her very important point. "Okay."

She suddenly wondered where he was on the Olivia thing. It *had* just happened. "You must really want to—" she jabbed her finger in the air "—stick it to your ex."

He chuckled. "Guess I'm not that vengeful. I'm more the type to cut someone out of my life and never look back."

"Not true. You looked back to Olivia." Not that the lying cheating bitch deserved him.

He smiled ruefully. "Guess I'm the forgiving type too. Maybe I was at a place in my life where I was ready for a relationship, and it just seemed like an easy fit."

Ding, ding, ding! We have a winner! "Why were you ready for a relationship now?"

He walked around her and took the seat next to her at the island. "Because before I was working my ass off, and now I can see the light at the end of the tunnel, finally making it. I guess my mind just jumped to the next step. I've got one of those analytical brains that organizes and implements."

"I guess that makes sense. Things are falling in place for you at work, and now you're ready to get your personal life in order."

He inclined his head. "It wasn't that well thought out, but, yeah, something like that. So how about you? You want to stick it to your ex?"

She slapped the island counter. "Absolutely. I'd love to send *him* a wedding invitation. You know he sent me one? That's what spurred me to write my goodbye commitment-phobe article."

"So vengeful," he teased.

"A revenge wedding," she said, a new idea taking hold. "Let's get fake married."

He tilted his head. "Come again?"

She blustered on, her enthusiasm building. This was just like what her friends had suggested with the fake fiancé and would surely bring her close enough to Logan to make a move. After all, a fake wedding should have a fake honeymoon. "If we get fake married, it'll fix my rep as a flaky, *lonely* relationship counselor and be a big FU to our exes. There's so much gossip speculating about our relationship already. Wouldn't that be so fucking—" *Oops!* The fucking had slipped out. She was getting ahead of herself. First kissing, then fucking. She stared at his mouth; his lips looked so damn kissable. His neatly trimmed light brown beard was driving her crazy, imagining what it would feel like against her fingers, her lips, her bare body. A hot shiver ran through her at the thought.

He was quiet. Maybe he was confused since she'd never quite finished her sentence before. Her gaze dropped to the open top of his dress shirt revealing a hint of manly chest. "I meant, faking great," she said. "It could be great to fake. And fun!"

She finally met his eyes, intent on hers, and licked her lips. "*Really* fun."

He turned her swivel stool to face him, his eyes suddenly hot on hers. Her stomach dipped, heat rushing through her. His voice was low and deep. "You realize a fake revenge wedding comes with strings attached."

She stared at his mouth. "Yes," she breathed. "A fake honeymoon."

His lips curved into a slow sexy smile.

She stopped breathing.

His hand slid under her hair, cupping the back of her neck and pulling her in. His words ran hot over her lips. "Sabrina, are you propositioning me?"

12

"I'm trying," Sabrina whispered, clear desire in her eyes.

A hot rush of lust surged through him. That was the signal he needed. "Then I accept." He kept her close, his hand cupping her warm neck. "Fake everything, but this part right here is very, very real." He brushed his lips across hers once and then again. Her lips parted on a sigh.

He held her jaw with his other hand, keeping her in place as he deepened the kiss, his tongue sweeping inside. He nearly groaned, her taste minty, her lips yielding and soft. Electric heat shot through his veins, the intensity catching him by surprise. The kiss turned wild, his doing, but she was right there with him, returning the kiss with equal passion. Fever hot. Every nerve firing. Her sweet scent, her taste, he needed to kiss more of her, *all* of her.

She moaned deep in her throat, an erotic sound that made him rock hard. Need pulsed through him, a primal instinct. He wanted her under him, wanted to bury himself deep inside. He'd never wanted anyone like this just from a kiss. He had to slow it down.

With every ounce of willpower he had, he broke the kiss, sliding his hand from her jaw to hold her throat. "I like that sound."

Her brown eyes were hazy with lust. Her voice was a

whisper, her lips grazing his as she leaned close. "More, please."

Oh, God, she was just so sweet with the *please*. He felt like a beast, nearly vibrating with need, straining to control himself. He loosened his hold on her throat, sliding his finger down it, staring at the rapidly beating pulse in her neck. She wanted him, but she kept her hands to herself, which told him slow was definitely the way to go.

He slid his hand from her neck up to her hair, gripping it and tilting her head back. He pressed his lips to her throat, her skin warm and soft, her taste glorious as he worked his way up to her ear. "Tell me you want me, Sabrina." He needed the words.

"I've wanted you for so long."

He jolted and met her eyes. *For so long?*

She grabbed his head and kissed him roughly, hungrily. *Yes!* His hands went to her waist, yanking the shirt out of the waistband, desperate to feel skin.

She tore her mouth away and pulled her shirt over her head. His mouth went dry. Red lace bra cupping gorgeous breasts. He needed all of her pressed against all of him. Like right now.

He didn't hesitate, quickly moving to stand in front of her and pull her up off the island stool and into his arms, soft curves pressed against him as he sealed his mouth over hers. Now her hands were on him, running over his shoulders and down his back. Thank God. He didn't even care where she touched him as long as she did.

He turned them, backing her up to the wall, kissing her long and deep, pressing his entire body against her, the ache to have her fierce. He eased back to pull the cup of her bra down, stroking one finger over her hard nipple. She moaned into his mouth, igniting him. He bent and took her breast into his mouth, suckling hard. Her fingers speared into his hair, holding him close as she keened deep in her throat. The sexy sounds drove him on. *More, more, more.*

He straightened, his mouth crashing over hers. Her hands slid up the front of his dress shirt, her fingers fumbling over the top button. He pushed her hand away, working it himself. Too many damn buttons on his shirt to get it off fast enough. She tugged his belt buckle. *Yes!* Just the important stuff. He left his shirt and undid her pants, yanking them down, panties with them, and bent to get her ankles free of them, catching the scent of her arousal. He nearly came right there.

He stood and gripped her hair, his mouth claiming hers as his fingers delved between her legs. She was hot, so fucking wet. He stroked her up and down, and she clutched his shoulders, arching against his hand. He made a lazy circle, slowly zeroing in, and she gasped into his mouth as he finally hit ground zero. Her hips moved rhythmically, seeking more of his touch. He slid his fingers down her in one smooth stroke and then inside her. So tight. *Fuck, fuck, fuck.*

He lifted his head, working hard to restrain himself. She was flushed with heat, breathing hard, her lips wet and swollen from his kiss. He slid his fingers from her, and she let out a mewl of protest, grabbing his wrist and putting his hand firmly back between her legs.

He groaned. "Sabrina, I want you so fucking bad. Push back at me if I'm too much."

Her voice came out hoarse. "You feel how wet I am. Fuck me right now or I'm going to scream."

His control snapped. His mouth slammed over hers, his fingers thrusting inside, pumping into her, his thumb stroking fast over pleasure central. She moaned into his mouth, and then her nails dug into his shoulders, her hips arching, seeking more of his touch. But it wasn't enough. He needed to be inside her, needed to feel her come when he was buried deep.

He tore his mouth away. Her eyes flew open and she ground against his hand. "I'm so close, Logan. Don't stop."

"I want to feel you come when I'm inside you," he half growled in her ear.

She shivered. "Hurry."

He grabbed a condom from his wallet, freed himself, and rolled it on in a flash. No time to strip properly. He had to have her now. He lifted her, the heat and scent of her overwhelming his senses, and he slid home, easing inside her tightness. Her body gripped him like she was claiming him. *Fuck.* He got even harder, slowly pumping in and out, trying not to be the beast he was, because all he wanted to do was slam into her again and again.

He slid a hand between them, stroking her hot wet sex. Her head dropped back, keening sounds from deep in her throat making him crazed with need. He kept stroking her, faster and harder as he pumped deep. She bucked against him, squeezing him, chanting his name. Fuck, he couldn't hold back much longer. And then she jerked, her body clamping tight around him, crying out. He pumped harder, stroking softer now with his fingers, keeping her right on the edge.

He shifted to whisper directly in her ear. "Come for me." He bit down on the cord of her neck. She jolted and then whimpered as he drove her on, thrust and stroke, thrust and stroke.

"Logan," she whispered fiercely, her body gripping him tight and then squeezing him rhythmically. About to go over. *Yes. Fuck yes.*

He thrust through her release, deep and hard, the sound of her exultant cry filling his ears as she came. Finally he let go—an explosion of light behind his eyes, a white-hot surge of pleasure as he pumped, shuddering against her until he was finally spent.

A long moment later, he held her jaw and kissed her, a slow, deep kiss. Not ready to let her go yet, he broke the kiss, his gaze following his hand as he stroked her heated cheek, then her neck and over her bare shoulder, loving that he could touch her like this now.

He smoothed her hair back from her face. "Is it bad that I just want to spend the whole weekend doing dirty things to you?"

She smiled, a slow, satisfied smile that filled him with joy. "It is our honeymoon, but I'm not sure you have the stamina."

"Oh, yeah?" He nipped her lower lip and then sucked. "Try me."

She licked her lips, her eyes hot on his, her hair mussed from his hands. *Fuck me, I want her again.*

Too soon. He lifted her off him and set her on her feet, holding her by the arms to keep her steady. He couldn't resist touching her more, smoothing his hands down her sides and over her hips before framing her face with his hands. "Before, you said you weren't starting to think about you and me. What changed? Is this just because the wine made you horny and I'm the only available man?"

She threw her arms around his neck, pressing her entire body against him. "You are the hottest man who ever graced this planet. And that's not the wine talking."

He couldn't help his wide smile. No question she was into him. He wrapped his arms around her, slid his hands to her ass and squeezed.

She spoke against his lips, her voice soft. "I want everything with you."

Everything. His dirty mind immediately flashed to all the ways he wanted to have her. He groaned and held her tight to him. "I want that too." He pulled away. "Give me one hour." He dealt with the condom, tucking it back in the wrapper, and got his pants back in place. "Be right back."

She blew him a kiss, smiling, naked and so fucking sexy. His chest ached at the beautiful sight. He gave her a hard kiss, turned, and headed upstairs before he gave himself away. Because he was feeling way too much for where they were at. Sex did not mean love. It couldn't possibly have happened that fast for him. He hadn't even known Sabrina wanted him. They'd been friends. Her soft admission played through his mind. *I've wanted you for so long.*

He headed for the master bedroom with its en suite bathroom, feeling a little light-headed. Probably from the stress of the day. His business meeting with Elias, his cheating ex, and tonight's unexpected conclusion would've been a lot for a week, let alone a day.

He flicked on the light and stopped short. Sabrina's suitcase was right next to his.

This hadn't been his lust driving everything. She'd *planned* to seduce him. Why else would she have set herself up in his bedroom?

One corner of his mouth lifted. This was going to be a dirty, dirty weekend. No holding back. He was going to make her as crazy as she made him. He firmly pushed all the earlier mushy stuff from his mind. That was just a side effect of wine, lust, and stress. A mind-fuck cocktail for sure.

Later that night, Sabrina walked upstairs with a quiet Logan, telling herself just to relax and enjoy. This was not the time to think about anything stupid like ruining their friendship or worrying about where his head was at with his ex. They'd watched TV for a short while, but he couldn't stop touching her, and she couldn't stop touching him—despite both of them being dressed again—and they mutually agreed the king-size bed would be better than the sofa.

He strode into the bedroom first, turning on the nightstand light. "Found your suitcase in here earlier. Looks like you planned to seduce me." He turned and grinned. His shirt was all the way unbuttoned, her doing. She'd been dying to run her hands over his bare chest. The cuffs were unbuttoned and rolled up, exposing muscular forearms.

She practically floated over to him, wrapping her arms around his neck. Now he smelled like woodsy cologne and sex, a potent combination. "Yep."

He flashed a smile that lit up his gorgeous face, his big hand cradling her jaw. "It totally worked." He kissed her passionately, his arm banded around her waist, pressing her tight against him.

Her body hummed with need. His mouth claiming hers, his hard erection pressing into her belly, his hand sliding from her ass to between her legs—all of it made her wild for him. She grabbed at his shirt, pulling it off his shoulders and then off. She was still dressed, but she couldn't help pressing herself against all that hotness.

He spoke against her lips. "I can feel your heat right through your clothes. You're so hot for me."

"So wet for you," she returned.

His dark eyes gleamed, his fingers pressing firmly between her legs.

She had to have him *now*. "I need you inside me."

His eyes dilated, raw need blazing from them. He scooped her up, cradled in his arms, surprising her.

She nuzzled into his neck, loving the feel of his soft beard and warm skin. He pulled back the covers and gently set her down. She waited for him to pounce for another hard and fast fuck like before, but he wasn't in a hurry. He slowly pulled the belt from his dress pants, setting it on the nightstand, and then unbuttoned his pants. She'd waited long enough. She sat up, grabbed his shoulders, and yanked.

He fell on top of her with a laugh.

"You're almost the way I want you," she said, smiling. "Just about six inches to the left and in."

"Shoes." He got off her, pulled her flats off and tossed them. Then he sat on the edge of the mattress and undid the laces on his dress shoes.

Slow, slow, slow. She'd waited frigging long enough.

"Logan, you suck at this! I want the fucking part not the shoes part."

He slipped off his shoes and crawled over her, his palms on either side of her head. "And to think I was waiting for a clear signal from you before." He gazed at her for a long hot moment.

Her lips parted, the need clawing at her, held under him but not having him. "Please."

His lips met hers in a firm kiss. *Yes, yes, yes.* She opened for him, and he took full advantage, his mouth claiming her the way her body desperately needed. She arched her hips up, a silent invitation for more.

He sat back, pulling her up with him. "Take your shirt off," he ordered while he stood to strip.

She pulled her shirt off and tossed it to the floor. Then she undid the front clasp of her bra and tossed that too.

"You're so beautiful, Sabrina. Touch yourself." His gaze was glued to her breasts while he finished stripping.

She cupped her breasts and stroked her thumbs over her nipples, a ripple of pleasure bringing her eyes to half-mast.

"Yeah, baby, that's good. Keep doing that." She had only a moment to take in the muscular hard planes of his chest and abs, his huge erection waiting for her—the man was hung—before he grabbed her by the hips and yanked her down to lie flat on her back. She squeaked in surprise and then moaned as his mouth closed over her breast, sucking, a sharp tug of need following between her legs. She slid her fingers through his soft hair, holding him to her, her legs falling open. His hand slid up her ribs to her other breast, rolling her nipple between his fingers and tugging just as his teeth gently clamped on her other nipple. Her back arched, her fingers tightening in his hair. He switched sides, taking a leisurely lick across her hard nipple before suckling gently, almost teasing her now, his other hand caressing her other breast.

"Logan," she said on a low moan.

He slowly released her breast from his mouth, his teeth scraping against her, giving her a jolt. The moment he released her, she grabbed his shoulders, trying to pull him to her. "Now, Logan," she said fiercely.

"Wait, you horny thing." He got a condom out of the nightstand drawer and rolled it on. It occurred to her he'd been prepared with the condoms for Olivia, but she wasn't going to bring that up. This was *her* time with Logan after she'd waited so long. She took him in, a spectacular view—all muscularly athletic and hung.

"Logan, you're so beautiful you could be a porn star."

He laughed and leaned over her, biting her earlobe and giving it a tug before whispering in her ear, "Spread your legs."

She immediately obeyed, flat on her back, legs spread wide. But instead of taking her, he settled on his side next to her and slid his hand between her legs. "So wet," he growled.

She moaned, her eyes closing at the pleasure of his touch.

"How long have you wanted me?" he asked, stroking her lightly. Teasing her, stroking everywhere but where she needed him most. She arched up into his hand, but he kept teasing her, circling lightly. "Tell me and I'll give you what you want." He stroked up and down her lightly, almost but not quite giving her what he knew she needed.

She opened her eyes and cupped his face, his beard soft against her palm, and told him the truth. "Ever since I met you, I've wanted you."

His smile flashed white. "Sabrina, baby, I love hearing that."

She closed her eyes, her cheeks hot, and dropped her hand from him. She was immediately rewarded with a firm stroke that sent a surge of pleasure through her. Then he gave her a pinch, a white-hot jolt that made her body jerk. His mouth covered hers, his tongue thrusting inside just as his fingers slid inside her. She was fever hot, consumed by him, her heart thudding in her ears. He shifted his hand, grinding the heel of his hand against her. Her head arched back, breath ragged as he kissed along her exposed throat, his beard rubbing against the sensitive skin, keeping up a steady thrust and grind that wound her tighter and tighter.

She trembled, panting, on the edge of release. She couldn't find her voice to tell him, but he seemed to know, increasing the rhythm. His tongue ran along the shell of her ear, adding to the sensory overload. She moaned softly.

He pressed his lips to the sensitive spot below her ear, and her fingers fisted in the sheets. His voice was low and deep in her ear. "Watching you get off is getting me so hard."

She exploded, rocking against his hand. He kept going, gentling his touch, bringing more waves of pleasure until she stilled. He held her firmly between the legs as the world came back into focus. She pushed his hand away, and he stroked her inner thigh.

She turned her head, smiling at him, so satisfied, so happy. "Your turn, beautiful man."

He rolled on top of her, slowly pushing inside. Even after their first time, she was still tight.

His hand came up to her jaw and pressed. "Open."

She opened for him. His mouth claimed hers at the same time as his body did in one hard thrust, the shock of it muted by his kiss. He was buried deep within her, not moving, just kissing her deeply. Something in her broke open in that moment, raw emotion that would've shaken her up, but the way Logan claimed her, buried deep inside her, the heat and weight of his body pressed against hers, she surrendered to it, possessed by him, at one with him.

He lifted his head, his gaze locked on hers, something deep passing between them. "Sabrina," he said gruffly, and then he started to move, slow deep thrusts that built pleasure within her again. She wrapped her legs around him, hanging on tight, her body clasping him with every thrust.

He grabbed her hip, tilting her up, thrusting deeper, harder, faster until he was pounding into her. Their sweat-soaked skin slapped together, raw and animal. She closed her eyes, her breath ragged, lost in a dark clawing need that threatened to break her.

"Sabrina, look at me."

She met his dark heated eyes. His expression was fierce, breath harsh, merging with her. She broke on a low scream, an explosion of sensation ripping through her. He pumped into her again and again, rocking her with more shock waves of pleasure before his own release on a low groan. He collapsed on top of her.

Still shaky, her legs quivering, she hugged him tight to her.

After a few moments, he lifted his head and kissed her, his hand holding her jaw. He lingered for a longer kiss, gentler now in the aftermath. He broke the kiss, gazing down at her, stroking her hair back from her face and then cupping her cheek.

She leaned into his palm and smiled. "That was amazing."

He gazed at her for a long moment, his expression unreadable before he looked away. Then he pulled out and rolled to the mattress beside her.

She reached for him, but he got out of bed, saying, "Give me a minute."

For a moment she panicked he was giving her the cold shoulder, but then he went into the bathroom, and she decided everything was fine. He was just dealing with the condom.

She curled onto her side, sleepy and warm. She couldn't remember ever feeling like this, so satisfied, so content. Logan cared about her. He looked into her eyes when they made love; he gave her pleasure before taking his own. He was wonderful. Pure happiness stole through her. Tangled up in this mess of a trashed career and fake marriage, it was sheer happiness that shined through it all.

Logan dealt with the condom, and then he just stood there in the bathroom, needing some space. There'd been a moment, more than one, actually, looking into Sabrina's eyes, where he'd felt something so strong his throat closed up with emotion. He couldn't pretend it was the wine, which had worn off hours ago, or just lust because he knew what that felt like and it wasn't this. It didn't make sense, though, the speed of it all.

Too tired to figure anything out, he made his way back to the bedroom, turned off the light on the nightstand, and joined her in the bed, rolling to his side, tucking himself behind her, and wrapping an arm around her waist.

He smoothed her hair out of his way and nuzzled into her neck, unable to resist her soft sweetness. "You always smell like honey and flowers."

"It's honeysuckle soap. I love the scent."

He ran his tongue along the line of her neck, tasting it. Then he remembered another interesting thing she'd said about him, and he couldn't resist teasing her. "Who's the hottest man who ever graced this planet?"

She wiggled her bottom into him but didn't reply.

"You're the hottest woman I've ever slept with."

She stiffened. "Really?"

"Yup."

"Olivia is very beautiful."

He pressed his lips to the sensitive spot below her ear. "Olivia who?"

"Still think I'm an untouchable porcelain doll?" He could hear the smile in her voice.

"Nope." He ran a hand over the curve of her hip, loving the feel of her, her skin like warm satin, smooth and soft. "Turns out you're very touchable."

She hummed a happy sound before looking at him over her shoulder. "I like our revenge," she whispered.

"What revenge?"

She turned back, quiet.

"Sabrina?"

A horrible thought occurred. Had all this fucking just been some kind of revenge against her ex? She had been upset about her ex before.

And here he was getting all mushy about her.

On the other hand, it wasn't like Sabrina to be confrontational and vengeful. Actually...she had confronted Olivia. And didn't she want a revenge wedding? And he'd said yes. Well, why not pretend? It *would* be a great FU, it would fix her rep, and he was already liking the honeymoon. They had the whole day tomorrow before she had to fly home.

California was like an oasis just for them. All sex all the time.

He'd deal with reality once they got home.

13

———

Sabrina woke naked, alone in a strange bed. Which hotel, LA or San Diego? She rolled to her side, away from the bright sunlight stabbing her eyes through the blinds, and shoved her hair out of her face, getting her ring tangled in it. *Ouch.* She carefully pulled her fingers out of the tangle in her hair. Wait a minute. She didn't wear a ring.

She stared at her left hand, where a gold band was sitting on her ring finger. A wedding band. Her mind whirled. She and Logan had been drinking champagne at Claire's house and plotting a revenge wedding. Did they have a San Francisco quickie wedding? Did they exist? She rolled to her back and hollered, "Logan!"

A few moments later, he stood in the doorway in a blue T-shirt and worn jeans, bare feet, looking as relaxed as could be. "You bellowed?"

She held up her hand with the ring on it.

He held up his hand with the ring on it.

"Did I miss it?" she asked, slowly sitting up. She hadn't been that drunk that she'd forget her own wedding.

He crossed to her and sat on the side of the bed. "It's not real, just an FU like we agreed. Fake wedding, awesome honeymoon." He leaned down and kissed her cheek.

She stared at her wedding band, still not getting it. "When

did you get these rings?" Shit. Had he already had the rings for a secret plan to marry Olivia? Ugh. What had she done? She must be Logan's rebound. The worst. She wanted to shove him out of bed and curl into a ball.

He got in bed with her, sliding under the covers and sitting up against the white padded headboard, his legs stretched out in front of him. "Got them this morning," he replied cheerfully. "It's noon, sleepyhead. Guess I wore you out."

She blushed, which was ridiculous after all they'd done. She'd climbed on top of him in the middle of the night, waking him for an intense round three. In the dark, the passion had unleashed even wilder than before. His dirty talk had spurred her on, lowering her inhibitions. She had been well fucked and collapsed boneless in the sleep of the dead.

Rebound.

He took her ring hand and held it up, looking at the ring in the sunlight.

She pulled her hand from his grip and sat with her back against the headboard and the covers up to her chin. "Do you regret sleeping with me?"

"Much too late for hiding." He yanked the covers down and traced a finger over the swell of her breast. "You have my mark on you." She glanced down at a small red spot, from suction or his teeth, she didn't know. He'd touched her in every way he could, everywhere, and she'd loved every minute of it.

She swallowed hard. "You didn't answer the question."

He held her jaw, tipping her face up for his kiss. "No regrets."

She nearly collapsed with relief. She didn't dare ask if he was over Olivia. It was enough for now. Obviously he was willing to help restore her professional reputation with the fake marriage. She couldn't ask for more.

"Good," she said.

He pushed her tangled hair behind her ear. "You want to let your ex know we got married?"

Strangely, Kevin was the furthest thing from her mind.

She was over it—the jilted-bride thing, the clueless wedding invitation, the enthusiastic *my fiancée is awesome* follow-up email. None of it mattered.

She looked into Logan's warm brown eyes, her heart in her throat. She couldn't possibly be his rebound when he looked at her like that, so warm, so tender. She knew this man, and he was one of the good ones. She could trust him. She *did* trust him.

"All that matters is you and me," she said.

"So damn sweet," he growled, his lips meeting hers in a swift hard kiss.

She let out a happy sigh, stroking his beard like she'd wanted to for so long.

He grabbed her hand and pressed a kiss to her palm, his gaze intent on hers. "Let's text our friends. You tell Claire to put the word out to the press. Presto, Sabrina's rep is restored. Ready?"

She nodded. He seemed so enthusiastic about it, and he had taken the time to get them rings. It could only help, right?

He retrieved her purse from where she'd left it by her suitcase and handed it to her. She pulled out her phone and texted Claire while he texted his friends. Then she texted a group text to all of her friends. *YOU GUYS! LOGAN AND I GOT MARRIED!*

A flurry of texts chimed in, congratulating them. A few jabs for not inviting them to the wedding with a promised party for later.

"You done?" he asked. "Everyone knows we're fake married now?"

She slapped a hand over her mouth. "Oh, shit. I said we were actually married."

"No problem. I'll fix it." He texted rapidly. "I'll tell them we decided to go through with it today in Vegas. There, now everyone's on the same page."

They looked at each other.

She suddenly wanted to take it all back. She was just starting things with Logan, and this was going to add a huge complication to their fledgling relationship. What had she done? This had been a terrible idea with terrible consequences. If people found out it was fake, she'd be ruined even worse than she was now with half her clients gone. She'd look like a *desperate* relationship counselor, who was left at the altar and then faked a new marriage. The only thing worse would be her nutty family jumping into the spotlight to comment on their long history of noncommitted relationships. Free love and all that hippy stuff before it was even cool. Her stomach rolled.

She swallowed hard. "Maybe I should call off Claire."

"Leave it. That psycho counselor is still out to get you. At least this'll take the heat off. I don't mind helping you out."

"But I'm supposed to be committed to commitment. What if people find out it's fake?" She winced. "Sometimes my vengeful side gets the better of me."

He cradled her cheek, his thumb stroking it. "Let's just enjoy a little weekend honeymoon. Later we'll have our fake divorce when everything's back to normal."

Her stomach rolled and churned and threatened to revolt. Someone was going to get hurt, and she had a terrible feeling it was her. "Maybe we need an exit strategy for after the fake marriage. You know, so there's no hard feelings."

He dropped his hand and stared at her. "Hard feelings from a fake divorce?"

She tried to keep the worry from her voice. "An exit strategy would make clear boundaries for both of us. It's a big leap from where we were to where we're at now. Honestly, I need it for peace of mind."

He looked thoughtful. "How's this for an exit strategy? You can say I was secretly a commitment-phobe and you told me goodbye."

"But we're supposed to be married. Commitment-phobes don't get that far."

He rubbed his beard. "Okay, say I was a jerk with a wandering eye."

She pursed her lips. "It reflects badly on me if I chose a jerk."

"Then what?"

She looked at a point over his shoulder, deep in thought, before meeting his eyes, saying brightly, "We'll say you're already married, but I didn't know it."

"No."

"We'll say you're gay, but you didn't know it."

"No!"

"Well, what, then?"

His brown eyes danced with amusement. "How about we say you secretly fell in love with a woman and I asked to watch you get it on?"

"Logan!"

He gave her a sexy half-smile. "It wouldn't be the worst thing for me to watch."

She worried her bottom lip. They needed to think of something good.

Logan got out of bed, stood, and held his arms out to her. "Okay, counselor, I see where this needs to go. Close your eyes, fall backward, and I'll catch you."

Her eyes widened. "Like a trust exercise?"

"Yup. It'll calm you right down." He wasn't grinning, but something about his tone bordered on playful. Maybe because he was playing at psychology for her when his real expertise was tech.

She hesitated for a moment, but then she thought she probably would feel better, knowing he'd catch her. It was one of those things where the body gets the message and then the brain gets on board. It couldn't hurt, especially as wobbly as she felt right now.

She slowly got out of bed, naked, and his gaze immediately dropped to her breasts and then took a tour down her body. She jabbed a finger at him. "Focus. You drop me and it completely negates the whole point of a trust exercise."

He backed up from her a few steps. "Okay, ready when you are."

She crossed to him, turned, closed her eyes, and fell. And kept falling as Logan dropped her—

to the floor.

In slow motion.

And then he was on top of her, his forearms on either side of her arms, gazing down at her, a gleam in his brown eyes. He smelled wonderful too, fresh and clean.

She bit back a smile. He looked so pleased with himself. "That was the exact opposite of what's supposed to happen in a trust exercise," she informed him. "You're not supposed to drop me."

He grinned. "Slow-motion drop with a very satisfying result."

She pursed her lips. "If you're not doing it the right way, you shouldn't call it a trust exercise."

A smile played over his lips. "Did anyone ever tell you that you do things too much by the book?"

"I told you why. My family is nuts. It was self-defense."

He smirked. "The first step toward a solution is recognizing you have a problem."

"Great, now you're psychoanalyzing me." She wiggled underneath him. "Let me up."

"No."

"Logan!"

"Relax. You need to loosen up, not try to control everything."

She tensed. "You're trying to control me right now."

"I'm trying to kiss you right now."

"Oh," she whispered.

"You seriously didn't know that?" he teased, holding her jaw. Then he kissed her tenderly before shifting to nuzzle into her neck.

"Let's go back to bed," she whispered.

He stood, offering his hand to pull her up. "Better idea. Shower together."

"I've never done that."

He leered at her. "Great. Now I can make you think everything I do is completely normal."

She laughed.

He gave her a quick kiss. "Hopefully after our shower I'll have tamed the beast enough to show you San Francisco."

"Am I the beast in this scenario?" She smiled, kinda liking the idea. It was better than an untouchable porcelain doll.

"I'm the beast in all my lusty glory." He nipped her lower lip. "But you can be too."

"Okay, give me a few minutes of privacy." She grabbed her toiletry bag, dashed to the bathroom, and shut the door. After she used the bathroom and washed her hands, she called to him. "You can come in."

He got the shower running, and she took the opportunity to brush her teeth.

Logan raised his voice over the running water. "I thought later today we'd take a cable car ride, check out the Golden Gate bridge, walk around a bit, and then head to Fisherman's Wharf. Sound good?"

She spoke around the toothpaste. "Awesome."

"Awesome." He stripped out of his clothes, setting them on the edge of the long bathroom counter.

She bent to rinse and spit, and Logan groaned. Maybe she should've put some clothes on. But what was the point? He'd only rip them off.

"I don't know what I want more," he said in a rough voice, "you bent over the counter or against the wall in the shower."

She moved quickly, laughing as she got into the shower.

He joined her, his arms wrapping around her, his mouth sealing over hers. This was all that mattered. It was good between them, and she wasn't going to think any further ahead than that.

Sabrina had just finished putting her breakfast dishes in the dishwasher when Logan came up behind her, putting his arms around her waist and nuzzling into her neck. Heat rushed through her. His kisses turned to soft sucking and small nips. Need gathered in a throbbing pulse between her legs.

"Logan," she said on a moan. The intensity of his touch

was unlike anything she'd ever experienced. One touch made her melt, one kiss made her body hum, all of her consumed by her baser needs. Their shower had been more than an hour ago, a slow, leisurely exploration. It was like they couldn't be near each other without it turning lusty.

He turned her to face him, his hand sliding under her hair, cupping the back of her neck. He spoke against her lips. "I can't believe I didn't see what was right under my nose."

"I hid my lust," she whispered.

"Why?"

"I wanted your sexy body, but that's not enough."

One corner of his mouth kicked up. "It's a start."

"I thought you were a bad bet relationship-wise."

His other hand came up, tracing the line of her neck and along her exposed collarbone. "Judgy much?"

She squeezed his arm, his fingers still playing under the collar of her V-neck T-shirt. "Well, you never seemed to get serious about anyone, plus there was the issue of your mom not being around."

He dropped his hand and took a step back. "I have very little memory of my mom. I was four. And to be honest it wasn't a big thing. My dad was awesome; I had a houseful of big brothers to look after me and a little sister that was pretty darn cool."

"There may be some underlying issues." At his scowl, she raised her palms. "We all have them. Me included."

"Maybe, but I'm pretty happy. I suppose if I had to pick one issue, I'd say that the woman who wanted me for so long never gave me one clue that she felt that way." He narrowed his eyes. "We could've been hooking up six months ago."

She closed the distance, wrapped her arms around his neck, and kissed him. "Then we've got some lost time to make up for."

He held her jaw and kissed her, slowly backing her up until she bumped against the counter, his body pressing hard against hers. Oh fuck. Not here. There were windows; the whole downstairs was an open space. She tore her mouth away, and he shifted to her neck, his teeth scraping against the sensitive skin, his hand sliding between her legs.

"Logan, upstairs," she managed, breathless. "Please. Windows."

He lifted his head, took a look around, and met her eyes. "No one around. Take off your jeans. We'll have a quickie."

She smacked his shoulder lightly. "No." She slipped away from him and headed for the stairs.

"No?" he asked with an edge to his voice.

She glanced over her shoulder and saw him stalking toward her, a determined gleam in his dark eyes. She rushed upstairs, Logan hot on her heels. He caught up with her in the hallway, grabbing her around the waist from behind. She squeaked. His teeth closed over her earlobe, giving a tug. "I know when you're wet for me. Your breath comes hard when your body wants the same."

She throbbed at the words. "I do, I am. I just want privacy."

He turned her around, grabbed her hands, and pinned them against the wall. "Private enough for you?"

She glanced around. No windows. "Yes."

Next thing she knew, her jeans and panties were around her ankles, and then they were off. He stood and gripped her hair, tilting her face up for his kiss, his mouth claiming hers just as his fingers delved between her legs, stroking her to a fever pitch. Oh, God, this man. He knew how to get her there fast and knew how to tease her torturously slow. This was fast, too fast. She clutched his shoulders, her limbs heavy and weak. A whimper escaped swallowed by his mouth.

Sharp need clawed at her. She grabbed his ass, pulling him close, needing to feel him inside her, not his fingers. He got the message, stepping back and pulling a condom from his jeans pocket. "Take off your shirt and bra," he told her as he stripped down and rolled it on.

She did, her mouth dry, watching him, remembering how he felt full and deep inside her. In a flash he lifted her, taking her up against the wall, fierce and hard and hot. She panted, her nails digging into his shoulders, her head thrown back.

Higher, hotter, everything in her coiled tight and then exploded. He thrust through her release, bringing aftershocks before letting out a guttural moan as he let go, his teeth clamping onto the cord of her neck in a primal hold that electrified her.

A long moment later, he held her jaw and kissed her, a long, slow, deep kiss like he couldn't get enough of her. She lost herself, drugged by it, in a haze of lust and deep emotion. He broke the kiss, his warm hand stroking her cheek, her neck, across her shoulder and down her arm. She loved that he was so affectionate even after they made love. And that was what this felt like. Not just fucking.

He smoothed her hair back from her face. "I'm a beast. Screw San Francisco. I just want you back in my bed."

She couldn't help her smile. There was no question his focus was entirely on her, not his ex. "We should do a little sightseeing. I don't know when I'll be back here."

He petted her some more, stroking down her rib cage and then holding her by the hips. "Two hours of sightseeing and then I want you naked on all fours."

"That's specific," she teased. "Sounds like you've given this some thought."

He stroked his thumb across her lower lip. "Ever since you bent over the sink this morning."

"Then why didn't you take me like that here?" In the shower, he'd pleasured her in another way, sealing her undying love for his mouth forever. And she'd returned the favor.

He kissed her and spoke against her lips. "I lost control because I wanted you so bad." His hands slid to her ass and squeezed. "Now I'm planning ahead."

"I can't wait," she whispered.

He groaned and held her tight to him before pulling away. "Two hours." He snagged his clothes off the floor and swaggered toward the bedroom.

~

After they were dressed, both of them glowing and happy, she followed Logan out the door. They stopped in the driveway, where his black BMW was parked in front of her Jeep.

"Which car?" he asked.

"Jeep might be more fun."

"Sure. Mind if I drive it? Then you can focus on taking in the sights on the drive."

She smiled, touched by his consideration. "Sounds good." She dug around in her purse for the car keys. A rustle in the bushes made her head snap up. A large telephoto lens was aimed at them. "Logan," she said under her breath, "someone's here." Oh, shit. What if they hadn't moved upstairs? There could've been sex pictures of them splashed everywhere, maybe even video. She grabbed Logan's arm, dizzy at the thought.

"Hey!" he hollered. "Get lost. This is private property."

The lens lowered, and her dad stepped out to the driveway. Her gut clenched and she pulled away from Logan, heading for her dad. She and her dad were linked by biology only. He'd never wanted to be part of her life. Tall and lean, his dark blond hair parted neatly to the side, he approached slowly, camera in hand. She'd destroy that camera, but it was possible he'd already sent digital pictures to another device or online.

Logan rushed toward her dad like he was going to physically remove him.

"Logan! It's my dad."

Logan halted, his head whipping toward her in question.

She nodded, her lips in a flat line. Now she had to explain her paparazzi dad stalking his own daughter.

Her dad stopped in front of her. "Hi, Sabrina."

She held out her hand. "Let me see your camera. Did you take pictures of me and Logan?"

"No, I just got here." He showed her, flipping through pictures of celebrities. Nothing of her and Logan. He studied her for a moment. "You look really happy."

She ground her teeth. She had been happy. Now he'd turned a beautiful time to shit. "Been a while since I've seen you." The last time had been at her disastrous wedding four years ago. In a forgiving mood, all starry-eyed about being a bride, she'd invited him.

"Better circumstances now for sure." Her dad turned to Logan. "Hi, I'm Charlie. Nice to meet you."

"Logan Campbell."

Her dad nodded. "Yup." He turned to Sabrina. "Sorry for hiding in the bushes. I wasn't sure if you'd talk to me."

She crossed her arms. "How did you find me?"

"Followed the trail—your connection to Claire Jordan, Logan's investor meetings, your sudden wedding announcement. I was already in California."

"Nice detective work," she said.

He bobbed his head. "If I found you, it won't be long before everyone else does. Can I please take a picture of you as a married couple? It'll really help me out to get the scoop."

She clenched her teeth. "No."

Logan held up a finger. "Just a minute." He pulled her back toward the house, whispering in her ear. "Let's do it. It's a big FU to everyone on our terms. Once he has the scoop, we won't have any more paparazzi popping out of the bushes."

She scowled. "My own dad sells me out."

"We let him for a good reason."

"He's never cared about me. I didn't even know he was my dad until I was thirteen. He showed up again when my mom started making some headway in her career as an artist. He wanted to sell pictures of her with her art, and she was happy to go along. I actually thought they might get back together because he moved in for a few weeks. But then he left again. I owe him nothing."

"That sucks." He glanced over to where her dad was fiddling with his camera.

"My people don't commit."

Logan took both her hands in his and gave them a squeeze. "My parents didn't stick either."

"So we're both screwed up."

He smiled down at her. "I say we go for it. Give him a big cheesy smile and then go on with our day."

She looked over at her dad, who was turned slightly away, giving them a moment of privacy. Logan was probably right; a picture on their terms would be better than dealing with random people jumping out at them.

She called over to her dad. "Okay. One picture. We'll stand in front of those bushes. I don't want Claire's house in the picture."

"Great!" Her dad smiled, but she didn't return it. He was a user.

She and Logan walked over to stand in place. Logan slung an arm around her shoulders.

Her dad lifted his camera, focusing it. "Stand facing each other, look into each other's eyes, and smile. Sabrina, put your left hand on his shoulder so I can get the wedding band in the picture."

She was about to say *we're fine* when Logan turned her toward him, wrapping his arms around her waist and pulling her close. He leaned down, whispering to her, "Come on, put your hands on me like you like me."

She laughed and rested her hands on his shoulders. He smiled down at her, his warm brown eyes crinkling at the corners. He looked really happy, and that made her happy. A surge of affection for him had her smiling back.

"Perfect!" her dad exclaimed, the camera clicking away.

She snapped back to reality and turned to her dad. "You get the shot?"

He checked his camera and smiled. "Yeah. Nice." He went over and shook Logan's hand and then hers. "Thank you so much. This'll keep me in the black for a month."

Logan stared at him, his expression hard. "You've got the exclusive. I suggest you get it out there fast. We're going out, and someone else might get the jump on you."

"Absolutely," her dad said, nodding. "Thank you."

Her dad turned to go, but Logan grabbed his arm. "I don't want you stalking us again, clear? I don't care who you are, I'll call the police."

"We're good," her dad said, his gaze shifting away. "This is all I need."

"Hold on," Logan said. "I'll open the gate so you don't have to climb the fence again."

Her dad actually blushed, glancing at her before staring at the ground, waiting. He shoved his hand in his pocket, fished out a business card, and handed it to her. "In case you want to keep in touch."

She shoved the card in her purse, irritated. He was probably hoping she'd get in touch for the next big payday picture. "Bye."

Logan did the code to open the gate, and her dad took off at a near run.

Logan returned to her side. "That went better than I thought it would. Are you upset?"

She shook her head. "I just want to pretend that never happened. Swear to God if my mother comes out of the woodwork, I'll die."

"What would she do?"

"Try to get the spotlight on her and her art. Her work has fallen out of favor. Art trends come and go, and she never moved on from her favorite subject."

One corner of his mouth lifted. "I kinda want to see those erotic paintings."

She glared at him. "I'm glad you find my embarrassing mother amusing."

He shrugged. "I'm just curious."

"Can we please go sightseeing now?"

He held her by the chin and kissed her. "Absolutely."

Several minutes later, they finally took off in the Jeep. She really hoped that was the end of her family profiting off her.

14

Logan marveled over Sabrina. Now that she was being real with him, she was passionate with a snarky sense of humor. She didn't hesitate to push back at him, asserting what she wanted, so he didn't have to worry about steamrolling her. They had a real give-and-take, even better than their friendship, because now that she wasn't acting the cool reserved professional, being more herself, they were on equal footing. Actually, she had the upper hand, though she didn't know it, because he was way into her. The sex was amazing, she cooked like a gourmet, and the more he got to know her, the more he liked her. It scared him a little how much he felt so fast. He tried to rationalize it—maybe she was his rebound, maybe it was the fake marriage that promised a commitment that wasn't actually there. Whatever the reason, he couldn't deny he felt something...deep.

They'd had a blast sightseeing. He'd played tour guide, and when he'd realized how much she was enjoying herself, he dropped his two-hour decree and spent the whole day out with her. They'd moved freely through the city, no one bothering them, in their own happy bubble.

When they got back to Claire's house, Sabrina cooked him a fantastic dinner with no recipe. Thinly sliced beef with basil, angel hair pasta, and salad. He even ate the salad because she put all these tasty things in it, toasted almond slivers and pear slices with a homemade dressing.

Now he leaned back from the table, full and satisfied. "I still can't believe you made all this without a recipe. You should've been a chef."

She smiled. "I enjoy cooking. After you do it enough, you get a feel for what goes together and how long to cook stuff."

"I can barely cook a frozen pizza."

She laughed. "I'm sure you can do more than that."

"So you eat like this all the time? Gourmet cooking?"

"It's not gourmet. I save that for special occasions. Those meals take more time, as they should. Good things come to those who wait."

He reached across the table and took her hand, brushing his lips across her knuckles. Her lips parted, her gaze on her hand. "Is that your subtle way of saying I need to wait before I seduce you again?"

She shook her head, smiling. "I meant the meal." She glanced back toward the kitchen. "Though we should probably scrub the pots and pans before everything sticks, and when I say we, I mean you."

He laughed and gave her hand a squeeze. "Okay, I can take a hint."

"If I had more ingredients, I would've baked you a nice dessert."

He pressed a hand to his heart. "You bake too?"

She tossed her hair and batted her lashes. "My friends call me a domestic goddess."

"You totally are."

"I just find it relaxing. It's stuff I didn't have growing up. You know, meals from scratch, a cozy home, so I learned how to make that happen."

"I grew up in a cozy house, but we never ate this good. Now I've got a big house that's mostly empty."

"Maybe for you coming from a house crowded with people, you like having all that space."

He grinned. "I just thought it was because I was too lazy to pick out furniture."

She laughed. "That too."

He stood and gathered their dishes, heading to the kitchen. He set them in the sink and ran the water.

Sabrina followed him in. "Do you know how to wash dishes?"

He narrowed his eyes. "Please. You think I'm a heathen?"

"Okay, okay. It's just that before you put everything in the dishwasher."

He started loading it. "Yes, but I said I'd scrub the pots and pans, and I will." He finished loading everything possible into the dishwasher while Sabrina watched. "I got it. You don't have to supervise me."

"Watching you do domestic chores gets me hot."

He barked out a laugh. "I get the feeling you're using reverse psychology on me, counselor."

"It really does," she insisted. "Do the pots and pans."

He shook his head, not entirely convinced, but on the off chance it got her hot, he was totally going to seduce her as soon as this chore was done. He grabbed a paper towel and squirted some dish soap on it.

"Hold on." She dug around under the sink and pulled out a clean scrub sponge. "Here, try this."

He got to work. "So what kind of dessert can you make?"

She leaned against the counter next to him. "Let's see, I guess it depends what you're in the mood for. Cookies, brownies, flourless chocolate cake, chocolate mousse, fruit pie—"

"Whoa. Let's start with the pie. What kind of pie?"

"Whatever kind you like. Apple would probably be easiest to find this time of year."

"Yes, please. What else can you do?"

"What do you mean?"

"How far do your domestic goddess skills go?"

She shrugged. "Guess that's a matter of opinion. My friends like coming to my apartment. They say it always smells like cinnamon and vanilla, and the furniture is so cushy. I made the accent pillows and knitted the throw blanket."

His eyes widened. "I need to see your place."

"So after this…we're going to keep seeing each other?"

He stiffened, surprised she'd thought it was just for the weekend. Well, he had said they were having a weekend honeymoon, but he'd assumed they were both into it enough to keep it going. Fuck. He set the pot down and turned to her. "I think we should."

"Why exactly?" she asked softly.

He scrambled to think of something good without showing his hand. He didn't want her to know how hooked he was because if this was all just fake to restore her rep, he was in trouble. "Mutual pleasure."

She pressed her lips together. "Until…"

"I don't know. Let's play it by ear."

She nodded once, turned, and started banging around in cabinets. He got the feeling she was pissed.

"What?" he asked.

"Nothing. Just looking for a dish towel." *Slam.* "Not there." *Slam.* "Got to have them somewhere, right?"

He turned off the water, dried his hands on a paper towel, and caught up with her right after she slammed cabinet number five. He wrapped an arm around her waist and pulled her flush against him, sliding his hand under her hair and cupping the back of her neck. "Sabrina."

"What?" she snapped, definitely pissed, but she was staring at his mouth, her breath coming faster. She wasn't touching him back, though, her hands at her sides.

"I know we're doing the fake-marriage thing, but I told you this part was real." He brushed his lips over hers, coaxing. "Don't be mad." Another brush of the lips. "Just enjoy."

She sighed. "I leave tomorrow morning, and I just need to know where I stand. So once we're both back home, fake honeymoon over, then we'll still see each other because of mutual pleasure, as in fucking?"

He got hard, hearing her sweet mouth say fucking, but her brown eyes were searching his, so he gave her the truth. "As in more than fucking."

She wrapped her arms around his waist and hugged him.

The beast was back. He didn't want to hug her, he wanted to bend her over the counter and bury himself deep inside. He cared about her, but the intense need when she was pressed against him made it impossible to hold back. He wrapped her hair around his fist and tugged, tilting her face up to look at him.

She flushed pink, the pulse in her throat beating rapidly. He stroked his fingers down her throat, loving how she responded to him. He was about to lean down and run his tongue over that pulse when she spoke.

"The cabinet slamming was passive-aggressive of me. I apologize. From here on out, I'll be a better communicator."

He shook his head. "You're too damn sweet. Don't apologize for being mad."

She met his eyes. "I was mad because it sounded like it was just fucking, but, for me, it's definitely more. I should've said that right up front. I'm still kind of new at the relationship thing, but I *really* want to be good at it. In theory, I'm an expert, for other people, anyway, but for me not so much."

"So self-aware," he teased. "If this is you throwing a fit because you don't know where you stand, I'll take it. I don't need you to be an expert at this." He spoke against her lips. "I just need you to be with me." He kissed her, letting her know how much he wanted her, a demanding kiss that ignited between them. Her tongue tangled with his, her arms wrapped around his neck, keeping him close, her pelvis pressing insistently into his.

The dishes could wait. He didn't think he'd ever get enough of her. It should've scared him, but he was too far gone. He went for it.

~

One pretend day of married bliss was all she got before she had to fly home. Logan would be staying on until Wednesday for more time at his big investor's office. She told herself this wasn't goodbye. He'd fly home, and they'd continue in some new phase of their relationship. The problem was, she wasn't sure what that was. She liked him way too much, and if she was honest with herself, she'd been slowly falling for him for months now. Some part of her wanted a do-over with him, where she got to him before he was involved with Olivia again, before any of this whole mess with her in the spotlight. There were just too many added stressors on a brand-new relationship.

It was Sunday morning, and she was all packed. There was nothing left to do but say goodbye to Logan and drive her rental Jeep to the airport.

She stopped in front of him by the front door, tried to smile and failed miserably. "Welp, goodbye. I guess I'll see you back home."

One corner of his mouth curled up. "Don't sound so sad. I'll be home in three days. You can survive that long without me in your bed."

So, okay, yes, the sex was phenomenal, but she was a little concerned that it eclipsed everything else. Not that she didn't enjoy it. He was a demanding but generous lover, and it worked for her. Big time. But all this emotion was building up inside her, and she was positive he was not at the same place. She just needed a tiny hint that she wasn't alone in these deep waters. "You think we should keep pretending we're married back home?"

"Sure, no big deal."

"Maybe we should tell our friends the truth."

"Let it ride. We'll tell them once the dust settles and your rep is golden again."

Another thought occurred to her. "What if there's reporters snooping around? Won't it look odd that we don't live together?"

He laughed and gave her hair a tug. "You worry too much. I'm sure all the attention on us will die down. You don't have any more TV interviews scheduled. You'll go back to work, I'll go back to work, and we'll catch up for lunch or *whatever*." He winked.

"Whatever as in sex."

He held up his palms. "Whatever is what you make of it."

She let out a breath of exasperation.

He wrapped his hand around the back of her neck, pulling her in for a quick kiss. He dropped his hand. "Have a safe trip. I'll see you soon."

She didn't move, not quite ready for this golden time in California to end.

He swatted her ass lightly. "Stop giving me those big worried eyes. Seriously, you're killing me with these eyes. You know me, right?"

"Yes."

"You trust me."

"Yes."

"Then we're good. Now go before I have my way with you again."

She found herself smiling. He could always make her smile. He grinned, leaned down and nipped her neck, jolting her.

She left on a high note. All thanks to Logan.

~

She returned on a low note. Exhausted and jet-lagged, she parked at her apartment complex late that night. It was dark and cold. Welcome back to Connecticut in January! She got out of her car, opened the trunk to retrieve her suitcase, and screamed.

A reporter was standing next to her. She hadn't even heard him approach. It was the same guy from the city with the long black ponytail.

She glared at him and yanked her suitcase out, in no mood for this shit. "Look, I just got home from a long day of travelling, and I just want to go back to my apartment in peace." She slammed the trunk and locked her car.

The man stared at her. "So you still live here in your apartment after your marriage to Logan Campbell?"

She clenched her teeth. She'd suspected this would be a problem, but Logan had acted like it was no big deal. "I haven't had a chance to move into his place, but we couldn't be happier."

"Pretty quick marriage."

She ignored him and headed toward the sidewalk, pulling her wheeled suitcase. He kept stride with her. "Any comment on Willow Clarke's artwork?"

She froze. That was her mother.

He went on. "She gave me an interview at her loft studio. She had interesting things to say about you."

Bile rose in her throat. She just bet she did. She'd probably lined up a whole slew of interviews talking about Sabrina as a child, all the while making sure her paintings were in plain view of the camera. "No comment."

"She said you were a dreamy child always making up elaborate alternate realities." No kidding. What else was she supposed to do? She couldn't even have friends over. Her friends' parents wouldn't allow their kids near "all that smut," and even if they had, she would've died of mortification.

Sabrina kept walking. Her dad had sold her out. Her mom had sold her out. Next maybe her half brother would pose in his nude sci-fi body paint, talking about how odd he always thought she was. Irony.

The man's voice gentled, speaking in a conspiratorial tone. "Hey, I get it. My family's not picture-perfect either. Maybe that's why you became a relationship counselor. Willow said your family doesn't do commitment and it was a big surprise when you chose that career."

Her gut did a slow roll, but she managed to keep walking, keeping her gaze straight ahead and heading upstairs.

He stopped at the bottom of the stairs and called up to her. "Seems a bit fraudulent to bill yourself as a relationship expert, considering where you came from and the fact that you and Logan don't even live together. Was the marriage fake too?"

She raced the rest of the way and let herself into her apartment with trembling hands. She got inside, locked the door, and sank against it, hyperventilating for a few moments while she desperately tried to take a deep breath. Finally she broke down in big gulping sobs—all of the events of the past week catching up to her.

After a good cry, she sat on the sofa and tried to think through her options. She had Logan on her side, she had Claire, she had a lawyer, though the lawyer had done very little. And then it hit her—she didn't need any of them. What she needed was to confront that psycho relationship counselor face-to-face and end this thing. It had to be her behind this. She couldn't imagine why this particular reporter was stalking her like this, digging into her past so much. He was probably paid to do that.

She'd ask Lexi for help; she lived right down the hall. Lexi could make an appointment with the psycho, and then Sabrina could show up in her place. She couldn't imagine Tara would let her in the door otherwise. She pulled her phone from her purse to text Lexi, hoping she was still up. There was a text from Logan. *Get in okay?*

She texted back rapidly. *A reporter was at my apartment. Now he knows we don't live together. And my mom is giving interviews about me.*

Her phone rang. Logan. She answered, and he immediately started ordering her around. "Get my house key from Ben and go ahead and move in. Stay with me until this blows over."

"I will not." It was too much too fast to be living together. Their relationship would implode from all the pressure.

"Just to get the heat off you."

"I can't just move in," she said stubbornly. "We've only had one date. There's an order to things."

"Just for a visit. No big. I'll be home Wednesday night, and we'll come up with a game plan. We're a team now. You don't have to deal with this by yourself."

Her breath caught. She really liked that he thought of them as a team. She always thought the best relationships were true partnerships.

He exhaled loudly. "Is your silence one of those passive-aggressive deals?"

She pursed her lips. Look at him, throwing around her psychological terms. "No, I was just thinking."

"Nothing to think about."

"How long would I live with you?"

"I don't know. Until your mom stops blabbing about you in the news, and your dad stops selling pictures of you? Until everyone has lost interest in us as a news item?" He lowered his voice. "I read the interview your mom gave. Damn, Sabrina, it was bad. She got real personal about you."

She rubbed her temple. She didn't even want to know what her mom had said. Logan was on her side, and she'd be foolish to turn away what he offered. Looking like a happily married woman instead of a fraud with a troubled childhood sounded really appealing right now. "Okay, I'll move in."

"Awesome. Does that include cooking?"

She pushed down the pang of anxiety that he wanted her in his bed and in his kitchen in that order. "Yes, I'll cook. I cook every night."

"Damn, this just keeps getting better and better."

"I need to go. Thanks, Logan."

"No problem. Bye."

She hung up. It was after ten. She texted Lexi, who texted back right away. *Come on over.*

Sabrina cautiously opened her apartment door, peeked around to make sure the reporter was gone, and headed down to the end of the hall where Lexi lived.

She rang the bell, and the door sprang open to a smiling Lexi, arms wide open. Her brown hair was up in a ponytail, and she wore a long tank top with yoga pants like she'd just been doing her yoga routine. "Congratulations!" She pulled Sabrina in and hugged her.

Sabrina gave her a squeeze. "Thanks, but that wedding announcement was just for the press. Between you and me, we're not really married."

Lexi frowned. "Oh, sorry." She brightened. "Actually, I'm kinda glad because I was bummed I missed the wedding." She gestured to her dark green sofa. "Take a load off. Want some wine?"

"No, thanks. I just wanted to ask you a favor before I go to bed."

"Anything."

Her eyes stung. She had really good friends. They were her family that she chose. "Thank you for that." She waited for Lexi to join her on the sofa before filling her in on all the damage Sabrina thought Tara was behind.

"That bitch!" Lexi exclaimed.

"My feeling exactly. I want to talk to her face-to-face and put an end to this."

"But what if it gets ugly? She might use what you say against you. You said she threatened you with her lawyer."

"My lawyer isn't putting an end to it. I have to be the one."

Lexi leaned in eagerly, her brown eyes gleaming. "So what's the plan? You're just going to show up at her office?"

"That's where you come in. I'd like you to make an appointment in her Fieldridge office, whatever time works for you. She does some individual counseling. Then I'll show up in your place. She'll have booked the hour. That'll give me enough time to get in there and have my say."

Lexi's brows drew together in concern. "Maybe I should go in with you. Like a witness."

"No, thanks, I prefer one-on-one."

"At least set the recorder on your phone. For your own protection. Maybe she'll admit everything she's done and throw it in your face."

"Okay, good idea."

Lexi rubbed her hands together. "We'll bring her down. All that bad juju she put out in the world's going to bite her in the ass."

She smiled. Lexi didn't hesitate to play hardball. "I'm glad you're on my side, tiger."

Lexi clawed the air with one hand. "Rwowr."

"Let me know as soon as you can get an appointment."

"I will."

She stood. "Thanks. I really appreciate it."

Lexi squinted up at her. "What's going on with Logan? We

were all so happy for you. It just seemed natural that one day your friendship would become something more."

She flopped down in her seat again. "I don't know. It's been so crazy." She filled her in on the whole Olivia situation right down to her and Logan getting it on that very night.

Lexi elbowed her. "Get it, girl."

She sighed. "And the whole fake-marriage thing was to help restore my reputation, but now I so regret it because it's made all these complications for what's just the early tentative stage of our relationship."

Lexi grabbed her phone from the coffee table and scrolled over to Sabrina's embarrassing text in all capital letters. *YOU GUYS! LOGAN AND I GOT MARRIED!*

"You sounded so happy," Lexi said. "I think it's fun. Besides, you've been getting to know each other for more than six months now. I'd say you're past the early stage."

"Tomorrow I'm moving into his house," she blurted.

Lexi smacked Sabrina's arm. "What!"

"Ow!" Sabrina scowled, rubbing her arm.

"I thought you said it was fake."

She filled her in on the reporter and her embarrassing mother. "He's just being nice, helping me out." She leaned in, finally voicing her real concern. "Lex, I'm a little worried. I think I'm in love with him."

Lexi gave her a sympathetic look. "Oh, sweetie, I know you are. You've been in love with him practically since you met. He's a good guy. There's nothing to worry about."

"There is!" All of her worries came out in a rush. "I'm new at relationships, he just broke up with a woman he was about to move cross-country to be with, there's a ton of pressure on us from the media attention, not to mention the pressure of suddenly living together after just one weekend of hot sex. He says not to worry, you say not to worry, but I worry, Lex! I know from my work how hard it is for couples to commit and stay committed." She rubbed her temple, the beginnings of a headache throbbing there. "I think I did this all the wrong way, and there's no way to go back and do it right."

Lexi patted Sabrina's arm. "Okay, I hear ya loud and clear."

"What do you mean?"

"I totally get being insecure about a relationship. Story of my life. That's why I'm done with them."

"I'm not insecure." Was she? She knew how much she felt for Logan, she was sure of that. And, yes, he was a good guy, but that didn't mean he felt as strongly for her as she felt for him. Oh, shit. Lexi was right. Everything else—all those other worries—were secondary. She was scared and feeling insecure because she was in deep.

She loved him.

Her heart pounded hard at the realization. Damn, Lexi would've made a good counselor too. "Maybe you're right," she said.

Lexi elbowed her. "Course I am. You'll settle down when you're more sure of him. And let me just point out, most guys wouldn't let a woman move in with them so easily. It says big-time relationship commitment."

She waved that away. "It's just until the whole mess blows over."

"If you say so."

"I think he just wants me for my cooking and my body," she said lightly, half-joking, half-worried. "He's like orgasmic every time I cook him a meal."

Lexi cracked up. "And for your body too!"

"Seriously, it's like I can't even talk to him without his hands on me, and it's an *embarrassingly* short time later before we're screwing again."

Lexi shook her head. "I can't believe I have to explain this to you, Miss Relationship Expert, but this is not a problem. Go nuts! Be happy!"

Sabrina sighed. "I am happy. I'm just...well, we'll see, I guess."

"How's the sex?" Lexi asked.

"Uh..." She hesitated to share the intimate details. It felt private what went on between her and Logan.

"Okay, okay, scale of one to ten," Lexi said. "One being ho-hum, ten being Fierce trilogy hot." That was the erotic romance series they all loved from book club.

"Gazillion times better than the Fierce trilogy," she admitted, heat creeping up her cheeks.

Lexi high-fived her. "Go, Logan."

"How do you know it's him? Maybe I'm the one making it great."

"Sure, okay." She smirked. "It's probably both of you."

It *was* mostly Logan taking charge in the bedroom, but still. Did her friends see her as an untouchable porcelain doll too? She should explain why she'd needed a quiet stable life, but she just wasn't up to it right now. The tumultuous weekend and travelling were catching up to her. "Okay, on that note, I'm going to bed." She stood and headed for the door.

"Last night as a single woman."

She stopped to look over her shoulder at Lexi. Her friend winked.

Sabrina shook her head, smiling, and headed out the door, hoping some of Lexi's confidence in Sabrina's new relationship would turn out to be right.

15

Logan returned home Wednesday night tense as all hell. And it wasn't because of work, which was going well, or that Sabrina had moved in for a temporary stay, it was what he had to tell her. He sat in his car in the garage, trying to mentally prepare for how best to deliver the news. He really didn't want to hurt her. The truth was, they were just starting as a couple, and he wasn't at all sure they'd be able to keep going once she heard.

All right, get your ass out of the car. He just had to tell her, explain the situation, and hope she'd understand. He was still in shock himself.

He left the car, grabbed all of his stuff from the trunk, and walked into the house. He stepped into the kitchen, half expecting it to be full of weird appliances and kitschy farm animal decorations the way a woman might decorate, but everything looked exactly the same. The dark gray granite counters were polished and free of clutter. It smelled good, though, like Sabrina had cooked dinner, some kind of meat.

He set his laptop on the island and put his stuff down. He was about to look for her when she appeared, her long dark blond hair up in a cute high ponytail, wearing a pink long-sleeved pajama top and pink flowery pajama bottoms. Bare feet and her toenails were painted pink. She looked like she lived here, relaxing in her pajamas. God, he'd missed her. Three days apart felt like forever.

"Hi," she said almost shyly. "I made pot roast."

"Thanks. I ate on the plane, but I could have some for lunch tomorrow."

She nodded, crossing her arms. A moment of panic gripped him because her expression looked a lot like the untouchable professional she used to be with him. Had she heard something?

He opened his arms to her, and she closed the distance, giving him a hug. Not an awkward hug, but a little stiff.

He pulled away and cleared his throat. "I need to talk to you."

She blushed. "That story was from Claire. She's been putting out the word through her contacts to counteract the bad press. You know, you and me happy newlyweds in our love nest."

He jerked his chin. Thank God for Claire. Sabrina's mom was still giving interviews and had appeared on a major news show this morning, a competitor to *Sunshine America*. He'd rather have no mom in the picture than a mom who profited off him like hers did. And the stuff her mom shared...no boundaries at all. Like that Sabrina had hung out with her stuffed animals the way other kids hung out with friends, imagining they were having fun slumber parties well past the age most girls moved on to real slumber parties. He read between the lines, imagining a young lonely Sabrina, but most people would probably just think she was strange.

"It's not about that," he said.

He took her hand and led her to the living room sofa. Once she took her seat, he met her eyes directly. "I care about you. A lot. I just want to say that up front."

Her eyes got shiny like she was going to cry, which got him choked up, because he could tell the deep feelings went both ways. Dammit. Things were just starting with them, and what he was about to say might finish them for good.

"Me too," she whispered. "A lot."

He blew out a breath. "Olivia got in touch with me today and told me she's pregnant. She says it's mine."

She slapped a hand over her mouth, her brown eyes wide.

He shoved a hand in his hair. "I swear I used protection, but I guess it's not a hundred percent. I was with her two months ago, so it's possible."

Sabrina dropped her hand. "Do you believe her? She did cheat on you. Maybe it's that other guy's. He's supposed to have an arranged marriage. Maybe she knew she couldn't get anything out of him."

"She heard we were married. I don't think that would've stopped her. I told her I want a paternity test. I found out she can get one as soon as next week, totally noninvasive. She does a blood test; I give a cheek swab. I'm flying back to California as soon as she can get an appointment. I just wanted to prepare you for the possibility."

Sabrina stared at him, her eyes wide and searching. "What does this mean for us? Are you going to move to San Francisco to be with her?"

"Not to be with her, but if it's true, if that's my kid, I want to be a part of his or her life. A big part. So, yes, I'd move out there for the kid, not for her."

She stood abruptly.

"Where're you going?"

She didn't meet his eyes. "I'm-I'm going home. There's no sense pretending we're married. She'll probably tell everyone she's having your baby, while you're supposed to be married to me, and the whole thing is so sordid." She crossed her arms tightly over her stomach. "Oh, God, I'm going to be sick."

She ran to the downstairs bathroom just off the kitchen.

He winced at the sound of her retching. This was fucked up. But what choice did he have? Never know his kid? His own dad had set such a strong example of what a good father was both to his own kids and all the other kids he took under his wing through the Police Athletic League. There was just no way Logan could ever be a long-distance father. He hadn't expected to be a dad so soon, but here it was, and he had to step up.

Sabrina rinsed out her mouth and headed upstairs to pack her suitcase, her gut still churning, chest tight, eyes stinging. She should've known it was too good to be true. Of course Logan would want to be a good dad, but to know he was going to be that dad across the country for another woman's child was more than Sabrina could bear.

She was glad she hadn't brought a lot of stuff with her. It made this all easier. As if saying goodbye to Logan could ever be easy. She went straight to his bedroom, where she'd expected to have more time in his arms, and now she just wanted to get away as quickly as possible. She pulled on socks and shoes, too worked up to bother changing out of her pajamas. She'd just throw her winter coat over it.

Logan walked in. "Sabrina, I know this is a shock. I'm still half in shock too, but it doesn't mean you have to go."

She struggled to get a deep breath. "I can't. I'm sorry, it's just too much." She put up a hand, trying to keep some distance between them. "It's not you, it's not us, it's just…the situation."

She wheeled her suitcase out of the closet and set it on the end of the bed.

"So does this mean the fake marriage is done or we're done?" he asked quietly.

Her lower lip wobbled and she bit it. "I think we need some time apart."

"I don't want that."

"I do." She quickly emptied her one drawer and tossed it all in the suitcase.

"Maybe you could move with me, if it comes down to it. Open a practice out in San Francisco."

She yanked the zipper on the suitcase, her vision blurring with tears. The zipper jammed, and she struggled with it, swearing up a storm.

His big hand closed over hers, pulling it away from the zipper, and pulling her into his arms.

She shoved at his chest. "I need to go."

"I don't want you to leave when you're so upset."

She lifted her chin, trying to be strong. "I'm fine."

"You're not fine."

A tear escaped and she wiped it away. "Okay, you want to know the truth? Before you told me your big news, I was working up the nerve to tell you I love you. There, I said it. I love you. And then you tell me you're moving to be a dad with a woman who never deserved you, and it *hurts*. Okay? I'm hurting, and I need to go so I can stop hurting."

"Okay." He released her and zipped up her suitcase for her, setting it by her feet.

She grabbed the suitcase handle and walked out on shaky legs, nausea rising in her throat. Not just because of Olivia and Logan, which was bad enough. Because he didn't say he loved her back.

~

Sabrina wasn't surprised to see the gossipy news sites breaking the news the next day about her fake marriage. Claire had spun it like Sabrina and Logan hadn't filed the paperwork, so it turned out the marriage wasn't valid, but fake marriage headlines were way more juicy. None of it mattered now in light of the Olivia bombshell.

Last night she'd made it all the way home without breaking down, took one step into her apartment, and bawled her eyes out. Then she texted all of her friends, telling them she and Logan were through and why. It wasn't just a break; it was a breakup. Her life had become the circus of her childhood, with messy relationships, children out of wedlock, and way too much drama.

She just could *not* go there again.

The next day, Friday, she turned off her Google alerts after a gossip site wrote a truly awful article about the love triangle between the Hollywood Love Guru (her), her fake husband,

and his pregnant ex. Only Olivia could've spilled the pregnancy news. Sabrina's friends would never have added fuel to the fire. Neither would Logan. But why would Olivia want the world to know she was pregnant from a man who was linked to someone else? It had to be pure venomous spite for Sabrina.

She dragged herself through work, not daring to cancel any of her remaining client appointments, no matter how bitter she felt about anything ever working out for anybody in a committed relationship. It shouldn't be so hard for couples. Love should smooth the way. But if there was no love, or unrequited love, then there was nothing.

She drove home from work on Friday relieved she hadn't run into Logan in their office building. She'd rushed in and out of the building and stayed in her office the whole day to make sure she didn't. He'd probably be flying out to California soon, getting that paternity test.

What if it wasn't his?

What if Olivia wasn't even pregnant at all? What if she'd lied to get back at Logan for dumping her? Or to get back at Sabrina for telling Logan about Olivia's cheating?

There was a way to find out. Why hadn't she thought of this sooner? As soon as she got home, she dug into her purse for the business card she'd tossed in there. Good thing she hadn't cleaned out her purse or she would've thrown away her connection to the one man who could help her, who specialized in taking sneaky pictures, who owed her for the big payday she'd given him with an exclusive picture —her dad.

~

Two days later, Sunday night, Sabrina had some photographic evidence. Her dad, still out in California thankfully, had sent her pictures of Olivia with Anil, the same man she'd been with for bathroom sex. And guess what they were doing? Shopping for baby clothes. She was definitely pregnant if she was shopping for baby stuff, and it looked like Anil was a real possibility for the father. In the picture, Anil was holding up a baby sleeper and Olivia was beaming.

She texted Logan the picture and called him, immediately telling him she thought Anil was the father.

He dug his heels in. "I won't be satisfied until I see the paternity test results."

"Did you have one?"

"No. She said she couldn't get an appointment yet."

Sabrina gritted her teeth. Olivia probably hadn't even tried to get an appointment. She was probably stringing both men along, enjoying all the attention and drama.

Logan went on. "I know it's not convenient to wait on a test, but she's going to be pregnant for nine months either way. And I'm not moving until the baby's born."

"Doesn't it seem like she's with Anil now? Maybe she told him the baby was his, and he wants to be with her."

"I don't care about him. I care about the kid."

"I know. I guess I just hoped…"

"I miss you. Come over or I'll go over there."

She was quiet. She missed him too, but this situation was out of control.

"Look," he said, "there's only two outcomes. One, the kid's not mine and everything goes back to normal. Two, the kid's mine, I move, and you have to decide if you're willing to move to be with me."

Leave her quiet, stable life? Leave her counseling practice that she'd built from nothing? Leave her friends who were like family to her? For a life as an outsider to another family? It would be just like when she was a kid—always the outsider—but worse because she'd have to deal with the fact that Logan would always be tied to Olivia.

"Sabrina?"

"What?" she asked softly.

"You said you loved me. When you love someone, you don't bail on them."

Her temper flared. "Do *not* put this on me. This is your drama."

"And you've had your fair share," he snapped, "which I helped you with."

She took a calming breath. "I want you to ask Olivia if Anil is the father."

"I don't trust her word. I want the test results. For all I know, she's playing both me and this other guy. But if she's shopping for baby clothes, she probably didn't lie about being pregnant."

"I thought the same thing about her playing both of you."

"And all of that has nothing to do with us."

"Yes, it does!"

"Agree to disagree."

She pulled the phone away from her ear and stared at it. Was he nuts? Did he not see the problem here? This was a huge fucked-up deal. She put the phone back to her ear just as he was saying, "It's been four days since I told you about this. I gave you some space, but shouldn't you have calmed down by now? Can't we just talk it through? Isn't that what you specialize in?"

A flurry of emotions slammed her at once—angry, indignant, utterly flabbergasted. Really? Calm down? Like she was overreacting to such life-changing news. And then he threw her counselor status in her face. *Isn't that what you specialize in?* Like she wasn't holding up her end of the relationship deal. He was the one who got someone else pregnant. Maybe. She was so confused.

He kept talking. "Maybe we need relationship counseling and *not* from you."

She gasped. "Who should we go to? The psycho counselor out to get me? That fits, actually, why not have a psycho advising me on my crazy life?"

"Did Lexi ever get an appointment with her?" She'd texted him about her plan to confront Tara before the Olivia drama.

"Yes. Next Thursday."

"I want to go with you. Not for counseling, just to make sure she doesn't try anything nasty."

She clenched her teeth. "No. I need to do this alone."

He exhaled sharply into the phone. "I told you we're a team, but all you do is push me away. You suck at relationships."

She glared at the phone, fury rising within her, and hung up. He'd gone for the jugular. He knew all of her history with her noncommitted family, her own lack of success in relationships, how much she really *wanted* to be good at a relationship with him, and then he twisted the knife in her tender heart.

You suck at relationships? Too damn far.

He called back, and she let it go to voicemail.

Love shouldn't hurt this much.

16

The only bright spot in Sabrina's life was an exuberant call from her literary agent a few days later. Her book had sold to a publisher for mid-six figures. At least she felt more confident that her practice would thrive again once the book came out. Of course, that was more than a year away, and her earlier enthusiasm for writing it had dimmed considerably. How could she be enthusiastic about committed relationships when her own relationship was such a disaster? She hadn't heard from Logan and hadn't seen him at the office either. Not because she was avoiding him. She figured he was done with her, tired of dealing with someone who sucked at relationships. But what was she supposed to do when so much was still up in the air? How could she move forward with Logan not knowing which direction his life was heading?

The day after her big book news, Thursday, she headed out for Lexi's appointment at psycho Tara's office. Sabrina had it all planned out what she was going to say. She was sure they could talk this through. They shared a common goal, helping couples stay together in committed relationships. She'd emphasize that her own book deal could never eclipse the great accomplishment of Tara's wonderful book, which was well researched and well written. Sabrina had read it in preparation for this meeting. And, most importantly, there were plenty of clients to go around, especially in this high-population part of Connecticut. Plus, Tara had a second office in the city teeming with troubled couples.

Sabrina showed up at Tara's office five minutes before the allotted time and took a seat in the empty waiting room. She was still in her work clothes, a pale pink silk blouse with black pants and heels. She figured her outfit would help project a professional image and keep their conversation on a professional level. She silently rehearsed her speech and then checked the time on her phone. Any minute now. She'd just clicked record on her phone when the waiting room door opened and Logan strode in.

She gasped. He looked like six feet of powerfully determined man heading straight for her. For a brief heart-pounding moment, she thought he might scoop her up, toss her over his shoulder, and take her back to his bed like a sexy caveman. Instead, he took the seat next to her without a word. She breathed in his familiar fresh masculine scent, all of her longing to touch him again. He was in his usual work clothes —long-sleeved black shirt, worn jeans, and sneakers. Her mind immediately flashed to the finely formed muscles of his shoulders and arms, his chest...and more. She shifted her gaze up, surprised at herself. Maybe after all they'd done, she'd never be able to see him again without remembering how he looked underneath it all.

She studied his handsome profile, his short light brown hair, his nose that tilted up at the end, his sexy lips, his neatly trimmed beard. For a moment she forgot why they weren't together. Then he met her eyes, his expression serious, and it all came flooding back. That was exactly how he'd looked when he broke the baby news to her.

"What're you doing here?" she whispered. She'd told him she wanted to do this alone.

His voice was low and deep. "I wanted to be here for you. Lexi gave me the time and place."

She ground her teeth. *Lexi, you will pay.*

She kept her voice low. "Get out. I'm supposed to be here for an individual appointment."

He whispered directly in her ear, "You don't know what this woman is capable of. She's been manipulative, vindictive, and threatening you."

She shoved his shoulder, but he didn't budge. "Go."

"I really do think we need relationship counseling," he said without a trace of humor.

"Well, we're not getting it here!"

The door to Tara's office opened. There she was, looking just like her picture, her blond hair styled in a layered cut, her angular face hard and thin. Her blue eyes shot fire. "You!" she spat, narrowing her eyes at Sabrina. "I saw your book just got a bigger advance than mine did. Don't even *try* to tell me you're not trying to squeeze me out."

Logan stood. "Hey, let's all just stay calm."

Sabrina put a hand up to Logan and walked over to Tara. The woman radiated pure venom, her blue eyes icy with rage. "Tara, I came here today to reach out to you, counselor to counselor. We both share a common goal of helping couples keep their commitment, and there's no shortage—"

"I'm the Commitment Counselor!" Tara slashed her hand through the air. "That's my thing. I trademarked it. You stole it. That's all you've been doing these past several weeks, siphoning off my hard work. Do you know how difficult it was to get where I am today? Now I look like a has-been, and you're the next pretty young thing."

"I'm sure you know it has nothing to do with appearances. Our work depends on our qualifications, our client satisfaction—"

"Oh, shut up. You're an idiot if you believe that."

Logan appeared at Sabrina's side. "Don't talk to her that way."

Tara's lip curled. "Well, if it isn't the fake husband with a pregnant ex. Thanks for making it so damn easy for me. I only had to pay one guy to get the ball rolling, and you two took it from there."

Sabrina jumped on that. "So you admit to paying someone to write negative stories about me."

Tara smiled, a wide evil smile. "Only a few, you did the rest just by being your stupid self."

Sabrina's temper broke her calm composure. "And you stole my clients! Offering them fifty percent off. I lost half of them to you! That's a serious loss of income."

Tara pursed her lips. "I'm sure your book deal will make up for that."

Sabrina scowled. "My clients are everything to me."

"Your clients are idiots," Tara scoffed. "I got them in here so easy, did one session, and told them they were cured. They left here thinking you'd been stringing them along for months for no reason. Except money, of course. Word spreads quickly. Have you checked your reviews online?"

Sabrina saw red, her hands in fists. "You bitch!"

Tara got in her face. "Ooh, you're mad now. Go ahead and hit me. This'll be the last nail in your coffin."

Logan spoke in a low voice. "Sabrina, no, let's just go."

She gritted her teeth, fuming. Tara flicked her fingers in a *get lost* gesture.

Sabrina turned to go, and Tara pushed her from behind, making her stumble. Logan caught her before she could do a face-plant.

Sabrina whirled. Tara was smiling like she'd won. Sabrina had never wanted to slap someone so much in her life. *No, rise above.* Big picture, she had everything she needed from Tara recorded on her phone, all the damning evidence admitting what she'd done.

"You'll be hearing from my lawyer," Sabrina spat.

She didn't wait for a response, hightailing it out of there. Logan followed close behind, shutting the office door behind them.

Tara yanked open the door, hollering all kinds of names at Sabrina, but Logan blocked the doorway, not letting Tara get to her.

"Go back inside, Tara," Logan said calmly. "This isn't going to help your case."

Sabrina stalked away, her adrenaline slowly draining from her, leaving her shaky. Tara didn't care about her clients. She only cared about the gloss and shine—her big trademarked self-appointed title and her bestselling book. She wasn't fit to be a counselor.

She moved in a fog, leaving the building and heading to her car, slipping into the driver's seat. The passenger-side door opened, surprising her, and Logan got in.

"Drive," he said.

"But your car's here."

"You can drop me off later to get it. I want to talk to you, and I don't want that crazy woman watching us from her office."

She pulled out of the parking lot, eager to get away from Tara. "I'm a little shaken up right now."

"You were a total badass. That should be your new trademarked title, Badass Counselor."

She laughed despite the dire circumstances. Logan could always make her laugh.

He gave her shoulder a squeeze. "I know you didn't ask me to be here, but I had a bad feeling about her. And the truth is, I thought it would be better if you had a witness to the whole thing."

"I recorded it on my phone."

"Me too."

She glanced over at him. "Thanks."

"Pull into that park up there, just past the light."

A few minutes later, she parked in the lot of a large empty park. The snow had melted, and everything was gray and brown. Fallow. Some people saw it as dead, but she'd always thought nature was hibernating, waiting for the glorious rebirth of spring. Being a cockeyed optimist was how she'd gotten to where she was in her career, the recent drama being very much the exception. Only somehow her optimism never carried over to her relationships.

Logan took her hand. "It's only been a week, and I miss you so bad I want to punch something."

"I miss you too," she managed over the lump in her throat.

"I know we don't have a conventional relationship with all the shit going on—"

"It's a terrible start for any relationship."

"Agreed. We need to go back to square one."

She was afraid to ask, the pressure on her chest making it hard to breathe. "Friends?"

He exhaled sharply. "No. We absolutely cannot be friends anymore. I know what you look like naked. I know what you taste like—"

"Logan!" God help her, she was getting sucked in. But what about Olivia and the baby?

He lifted their joined hands and brushed his lips across her knuckles, bringing warm tingles, his beard brushing the sensitive skin. "So dating, we need to date. At some point you'll trust me enough to get over your commitment phobia. I know that's the real reason you bailed on me."

She stared at him in shock.

He released her hand, watching her steadily.

Was it true? She'd thought she'd moved past that when she finally crossed the line of friendship with him. Oh, shit, it was true. She'd had one foot out the door the entire time. How could she ever expect to deeply connect when she was afraid to be dumped or, worse, feel unloved like when she was a kid?

"I'm working on it," she finally said.

"Olivia was an old love I needed to let go of, and I have, okay?" He framed her face with his hands. "No matter what happens, you're the one I want. You're the one I'm in love with, and that's not going away. It's deep and it's messy, but I promise you it is *real*."

She sucked in air.

He kept talking. "The love was already there, building between us as we got to know each other as friends." He kissed her, a swift hard kiss. "I worried it was too fast, but then…when you left, my house felt so empty. Cold and dead. Which doesn't make sense because we never even got to live together, but I kept imagining you there, cooking up a storm in the kitchen, curling up with me on the sofa, or warming my bed." His forehead dropped to hers. "Sabrina, you belong with me."

Her throat was tight, her heart pounding, her stomach fluttering because suddenly she could *feel* his love. It was deep and it was real.

"I love you," she managed. "I never stopped."

"You agree you belong with me?"

She nodded, tears blurring her vision.

"I love you too. I want you in my life." His voice choked, and that made her get even more choked up. He tipped her chin up, meeting her eyes directly. "Whatever happens, just be with me. That's all I need. The rest we'll work out together."

He didn't wait for her response, instead kissing her tenderly before pulling away, his fingers trailing down her throat. "I want you to move back in with me, but I can wait." His voice was husky, his warm brown eyes intent on hers. "I don't think it'll take long before you're ready to take it to the next level."

Her breath hitched. "Which is?"

"Marrying me."

She smacked his chest, her eyes welling again. "Shut up."

He held her hand against his heart beating strong and steady. "I'm serious."

Her fingers clutched his shirt. "But you said it was hard to imagine committing to forever when the odds are stacked against a successful marriage."

He loosened her grip on his shirt and took her hand in his. "When did I say that?"

"Before. When we were friends having lunch in my office."

"Ah. There's your answer. That was before we connected." He smoothed her hair back with his other hand and cradled her jaw. "Before I knew you were my soul mate. Before I knew how deep love can go, how strong the pull to be with one person forever. That's who you are for me, Sabrina. You're my forever."

She burst into tears, blubbering about the order of things, the uncertain future, and what was he thinking?

"We'll talk it out, all the messy details." He hugged her and wiped her tears before whispering in her ear, "Tell me when you're ready to marry me. I can't wait to start our life together."

She raised a shaky hand to cup his cheek, her voice quavering. "You'll be the first to know."

~

Logan flew out to California the Monday after his big talk with Sabrina, demanding a paternity test from Olivia and refusing to leave until they got one. Sabrina needed that peace of mind and so did he.

They got tested that day, and he flew home. Three days later, they got the results. He wasn't the father. Olivia confided in Logan that she hadn't known if the baby was his or Anil's, so she'd told both of them it was theirs to see who would step up. Turned out both he and Anil had wanted to be part of the kid's life, but all along it was Anil she loved. She also confided how worried she was because her parents didn't approve of Anil as a husband because he was Hindu, and his parents didn't approve of her because she wasn't Hindu. None of that fazed Logan. He was truly over her. So he gave her his best wishes and told her to let Anil know the baby was his and see what happened.

The very next day Olivia texted Logan a happy note that she and Anil had just eloped in Las Vegas. Logan was glad for her. Pissed she'd put him through all this, even knowing it might not be his, but ultimately he couldn't waste any of his energy worrying about what she did.

His future was with Sabrina.

EPILOGUE

Two weeks after what Sabrina now thought of as their love talk—when Logan had let her know just how much she meant to him—she happily showed up on his arm at the Clover Park Valentine's Day dance. Dating Logan was wonderful. They spent the night at each other's places on the weekend, but the rest of the time they lived apart. She hadn't realized how much she needed that stability and routine to feel secure enough to open her heart and keep it open. Two weeks of Logan's steady love, a short-lived fake marriage, plus months of solid friendship were all it took for Sabrina to commit. She could admit to being relieved he was no longer tied to Olivia in any way, but Sabrina's love for him was so deep, her commitment so solid, she now would've chosen to follow him to California just so they could be together. Fortunately, she didn't have to.

Her life was finally back on track. She was slowly rebuilding her practice, her lawyer had shut down any further defamation from Tara with the damning evidence Sabrina had recorded against her, and she was working on her book, *Romance Rebel*. The title was growing on her because she was a bit of a rebel the way she did her own relationship from the deep end and tiptoed on back out. She understood how deep commitment issues could go and had a new empathy for commitment-phobes. After all, she used to be one.

"You want some love punch?" Logan asked her, his hand sliding from the back of her neck down her spine in one smooth stroke, bringing a warm tingle along its path. "I heard it's spiked."

She smiled up at him, running a hand down his arm, loving the feel of soft fabric over hard muscle. He wore a navy blue suit that made him look even hotter than usual, all accomplished and professional. She'd dressed up too, wearing a dress she'd bought special for the occasion—it was tight and black, and Logan couldn't keep his hands off her in it. The dress had a V-neck and cute layered fringes at the thigh-high hem that went perfect with her silver winged heels. "Sure, thanks."

He gazed back at her tenderly before turning to her friend. "How about you, Lexi?"

"Make it a double," Lexi replied. "Thanks."

Logan inclined his head and went to get the drinks.

Lexi smoothed her hands over her hips in a dark blue satin cocktail dress and glanced around the crowded room, looking self-conscious. Sabrina had already told her she looked amazing. Her dark brown hair was up in a sophisticated twist; her dress with a white lapel along the deep V was super sexy. Surely, this would be a romantic night for Lexi. Love was in the air.

Sabrina put an arm around Lexi and gave her a little squeeze. Lexi hadn't wanted to come tonight, saying she didn't want to be the only single woman at a dance full of couples. When Sabrina had pointed out Hailey was going, Lexi had snorted, saying, "She's in a relationship with her dog."

It was hard to deny that. Hailey had spent the last month and a half in sessions with a dog trainer, coaching Rose to be a therapy dog for the sole purpose of having Rose with her everywhere she went. Not that she didn't already sneak Rose everywhere in her giant pink doggie purse, but she was eager to take Rose out of her purse more and let her explore.

Logan returned a few minutes later and handed over the punch. "I took a sip of yours," he said to Sabrina. "Strong stuff."

"Awesome," Lexi said and took a big swallow.

"I'm heading to the bar for a beer," Logan said. "Be right back." He left.

Garner's Sports Bar & Grill had catered the event, and she'd seen Josh setting up earlier. He'd brought staff with him and, surprisingly, had come out from behind the bar to mingle a bit. Maybe he'd even dance, though Sabrina had to admit if he did, he likely wouldn't ask Lexi. Not because Lexi wasn't a great person, more because he was drawn to a certain strawberry blond woman currently in love with her dog.

She focused on Lexi again, who watched the room with a grim expression. "Lexi, your time will come," Sabrina said gently. "Just be patient. Maybe it'll happen tonight."

Lexi sighed. "Truth? I think we had the right idea marrying ourselves. Who needs a man? I have a great career, great friends, a nice apartment, nice vacations, and…and… lots of great stuff. It's only weird when I'm surrounded by couples. No offense."

"No offense taken," Sabrina murmured. She knew how hard it was to watch all your friends find their forever love when you couldn't even move past the second date. She wasn't even sure if Lexi ever moved past the first date. Most men didn't pass muster with her.

Hailey waved at them and headed over in her deep red off-the-shoulder dress that clung to her perfect body. Red ballet flats with silk ribbons wound up her ankles. Even with her giant doggie purse, she still looked every bit the beauty queen.

"I swear," Lexi said, under her breath, "if Hailey tries to get me to meet someone one more time, I'm going to turn the tables on her. See how she likes it."

"She means well," Sabrina whispered.

Hailey reached them and gave them both a hug. "Happy Valentine's Day! Such a romantic day, right? It's too bad I didn't have any Valentine's Day weddings this year, though I wouldn't be surprised if some men are moved to propose tonight." She looked right at Sabrina when she said that.

Sabrina smiled serenely. "Maybe." She doubted Logan would propose, but she didn't want to lessen the romantic view Hailey had, however unrealistic.

"Holy crap!" Lexi chortled. "Check them out!"

They all turned to the dance floor, where Mr. Campbell, Joe, was slow dancing with Hailey's mom, Brandy. They were barely moving, pressed close together, cheek to cheek.

Sabrina and Lexi exchanged surprised looks. Hailey winced.

"I didn't know they were still together," Sabrina said. Last she'd heard, Joe had asked Brandy out. Of course, Sabrina had been a little out of the gossip loop with all the drama in her own life.

"It's all I hear about," Hailey said, rolling her eyes. She lowered her voice. "And she won't stop talking about how great he is in bed." She shuddered. "It's revolting."

Sabrina looked around for Logan and caught his older brother Josh's eye. She waved at him, thinking how nice he looked dressed up in a white button-down shirt and gray pants. His sleeves were rolled up to his elbows, exposing tanned muscular forearms, probably from all his bartending work.

He walked over to them, doing his usual slow amble, but the moment he got close, Hailey's dog erupted in ferocious barks, popping her head out of Hailey's purse.

Lexi leapt at the opportunity to push back a little at Hailey. "Let me take Rose out for a little fresh air. I could use some too." This was Lexi's devious way of letting Josh get close to Hailey. Otherwise, Rose would've prevented it. The dog really didn't like Josh, barking and growling every time he got near.

Hailey glanced out the window and back to Lexi. "It's cold out. Are you sure?"

Lexi smiled sweetly. "I'm sure. It's no trouble at all."

"Okay, thanks." Hailey handed over her doggie purse.

Lexi walked quickly away, and Rose's barking abruptly stopped.

Josh ruffled Hailey's hair. "Hey, little sis."

Hailey frowned and smoothed her hair down. "Do *not* call me that."

The three of them stared at Joe and Brandy, the happy couple lost in their own little world.

"My dad seems smitten," Josh said.

"It's nice," Sabrina put in. They both ignored her.

Hailey turned to Josh. "We have to stop this. My mom is a total flake."

"Seems okay to me," Josh said, his gaze returning to the happy couple. "And she's still looking fi-i-ne—"

Hailey spoke through her teeth. "Shut. Up. That is my mother."

Josh turned to Hailey. "You look like her."

Sabrina suppressed a smile. Josh was flirting. Would Hailey pick up on it? She was exceedingly dense when it came to Josh.

Hailey flicked her long strawberry blond hair over her shoulder. "Where's Clarissa?"

Josh turned back to the dance floor. "Probably facing east."

Hailey stared at the dance floor too before saying casually, "I haven't seen her around."

Josh didn't reply.

"Are you still together?" Hailey asked, not looking at Josh.

"No," he replied, not looking at Hailey.

"Oh." Hailey rocked back and forth on her red ballet flats. "What happened?"

Josh kept staring straight ahead. "The usual."

Hailey looked at him. "Not a good fit?"

He glanced at her and looked back to the dance floor. "Sure, let's call it that."

They stared at Brandy and Joe. Sabrina had to admit it must've been weird for them to watch their parents looking so in love. You just didn't expect it at that age.

Logan finally returned and slid his arm around her before taking a sip of beer. "Who's that with Dad?" he asked Josh.

"Brandy," Josh answered.

"Hailey's mom," Sabrina whispered to Logan, filling in the important part.

Logan glanced at Hailey and then over to Brandy. "Huh."

Josh turned to Hailey. "You realize if they get married, we'll be brother and sister. That's why I called you little sis."

Hailey gasped. "Omigod, don't say that!"

"Hey," Josh said, "I'm a good big brother. Ask my brothers and sister."

Hailey stared at him in horror.

Logan put in his vote of confidence. "He's okay."

Josh shot Logan a look like *shut up* and went about building his case. "Take Alex for one. I got him the nanny he needed, and now they're a happy little family."

Hailey stuck out her tongue, pretending to hurl.

Josh raised a brow. "Okay there?"

Hailey straightened like she suddenly remembered something. "You put your dream of owning your own bar on hold to put Mad through college. Why not let Jake cover it? He's loaded."

Logan hissed out a breath. Sabrina suspected she knew why.

Josh glared at Hailey, turned on his heel, and walked away.

Hailey's jaw dropped, watching him go. She turned to Sabrina, eyes wide. "What did I say?"

Sabrina spoke in a gentle tone. "I get the feeling he has a chip on his shoulder about Jake being more successful than him. They're identical twins; sometimes that comes with a rivalry."

Logan shook his head. "They're not rivals. They've always been close, but you're right about the chip on his shoulder over the money thing."

Logan's younger sister, Mad, walked over just then. "Hailey, I think we might be sisters for real soon. Can you believe our parents? I'll tell ya it's a lot better than when my dad dated my mom." That had been a strange time. About a year ago the Campbell mom had made an appearance, after so many years away, and briefly got together with her ex-husband.

"True that," Logan put in.

Hailey frowned. "I love my mom, but I think your dad would be better off with someone else."

"Why?" Mad asked.

"Because," Hailey said through her teeth. She reached for Rose and realized her doggie purse wasn't there. She looked around for Lexi, who wasn't back yet. Then she froze, staring at Josh, who was glaring at her from across the room. Hailey quickly turned back to Mad. "Why did you let Josh pay your college tuition when Jake could easily afford it?"

Mad shrugged. "He insisted, and when he digs in, I know he's not moving. It would've been an insult to turn him down, especially for Jake's money. Josh could've got in on the ground floor with Jake's company, but he took a different path. Now Jake's a billionaire and Josh isn't. Sucks for him, but he's doing all right. Josh is careful with his money."

Hailey looked thoughtful. "Hmm. Wait. If he could afford to pay your tuition, why didn't he ever pay me back the five hundred he owes me?"

"Maybe it was the principle of the thing, making you go get it." Mad smirked. "Maybe he just wanted to lure you back to his place."

Sabrina exchanged an amused look with Logan. They'd talked about Hailey and Josh and were in total agreement that their frenemy one-upmanship would only end when they either killed each other or jumped into bed. Either way was bound to be entertaining.

Hailey scowled. "Lure me back to his place or have a reason to fight with me, the cad."

Mad laughed.

"It's true!" Hailey threw her arm wide toward Josh, but refrained from pointing. "Look at him over there, glaring at me! All he wants to do is fight! He makes me nuts!"

"Breathe, Hailey," Sabrina suggested.

Hailey took a few deep breaths, composing herself. "Thank you, Sabrina, for the reminder. You ready?"

Sabrina smiled, reaching into her small purse and palming the needed item. "Yup."

"What's going on?" Logan asked.

Hailey slipped away, smiling mysteriously.

Logan held Sabrina by the chin, studying her. "You're looking mighty pleased with yourself."

"Oh, I am."

He kissed her. "I love you."

She beamed. "I love you too."

Hailey's voice rang out over the microphone. "Happy Valentine's Day, everyone! By special request, here is a song especially for Sabrina and Logan." The song began, Etta James's "At Last." Because *at last* Sabrina had the committed relationship she'd craved with the love of her life.

Logan grinned. "Just us on the dance floor, huh? And here I thought you wanted to avoid the spotlight."

"I kinda got used to it." She took his hand and guided him to the dance floor. "I actually like it when it can help other people. In this case, you."

He pulled her close, one arm banded around her waist, the other holding her hand in a very close waltz position. "And how're you helping me?"

She held her hand with her surprise behind his back. "I'm ready to commit to you."

"Yeah?"

"Yes." She pulled back from him a little and opened her hand, showing him her gift. It was a ring, polished rosewood on a cobalt black band. She met his warm brown eyes. "I want to marry you."

His smile lit up his gorgeous face. "Sabrina, are you proposing to me right now?"

She laughed. "Yes! Will you marry me?"

"I absolutely will marry you."

She laughed again and slipped the ring on his finger.

He pulled a diamond ring from his pants pocket and held it up. "Will you marry me?"

"Ah! We double proposed!"

He slid the ring on her finger. "Leave it to a relationship counselor to double down on the commitment."

Heart in her throat, she choked out, "I doubled down on you."

He held her jaw and kissed her passionately. She threw her arms around his neck and returned his kiss with all the love in her heart. The place erupted in wolf whistles and cheers. Logan broke the kiss and gestured over to Hailey, who pulled a rope that released red, white, and pink balloons from a net in the ceiling.

Sabrina looked up in surprise. "I didn't even notice them way up there."

"I had to do something romantic," Logan said, bouncing a balloon away. "Guess this means you're moving back in with me."

"Absolutely. Guess this means you're going to be my husband for real."

He pulled her close again, one hand holding her jaw. "You have no idea how good that sounds."

"Husband."

"Wife." He kissed her long and deep and tender. They pulled apart at the sound of applause and grinned at each other.

Hailey rushed over to congratulate them. "You guys, you have to get married on Valentine's Day next year. It's a Saturday and the anniversary of your double engagement, wouldn't that be great?"

Sabrina and Logan exchanged a look.

"We'd love to," Sabrina said.

Hailey squealed. Which was the cue for all of their friends to rush over and congratulate them.

Soon everyone was on the dance floor, arms around each other, swaying and singing. The love was palpable in the room with all the couples in love, even Hailey danced with Rose in her arms. Sabrina exchanged a warm loving look with Logan. She'd taken a chance on romance, a chance on him, and been rewarded with the kind of love she'd always longed for.

The single people were otherwise occupied. Josh was back working behind the bar, and Lexi and Marcus were having a low conspiratorial conversation in the corner.

A short while later, Logan pulled her off the dance floor, whispering in her ear, "Come on, Valentine, time for the naked part. I've got plans for you. Think red velvet rope, wrists and ankles."

She grinned and whispered back, "Think multiple orgasms. Mine."

His hand went to her throat, stroking his fingers down it, his gaze intent. "You're mine."

She cupped his cheek, his soft beard a caress against her palm. "And you're mine. Forever."

His eyes shiny, he growled, "I love you so damn much."

"I love you too." She blinked tears away. "I can't believe we both proposed."

He ran his hands from her shoulders to her wrists in one smooth stroke. "That's because you're a romance rebel." He winked.

She laughed at the reference to her upcoming book. "And what's your excuse?"

He scooped her up, cradling her in his arms. "I can't wait to start our lives together."

"Omigod, I'd swoon if you weren't carrying me."

"I know."

They grinned at each other and left for their own private Valentine's Day celebration. Their first of many wonderfully romantic, super-sexy, *committed* celebrations.

Dear Readers,

Josh and Hailey as brother and sister? Horror! Will their parents' newfound love bring these two closer together or will it be the ultimate showdown? Stay tuned! What do you think Marcus and Lexi were talking about in their conspiratorial huddle at the Valentine's Day dance? Maybe some devious plan. *Mua-ha-ha.* Next up is Marcus and Lexi's story, *Wicked Flirt*, book 9 in the Happy Endings Book Club series. Join the club and get your happy ending!

Wicked Flirt

When event planner Lexi Judson finds herself unemployed and desperate for work, she approaches the last man she'd ever want to do business with: smoking hot Marcus Shepard, bar owner and legendary player. But desperate times call for networking with panty-melting man candy.

The good news? He says yes to hiring her for a fantastic event.

The bad news? The job comes with some incredibly uncomfortable strings.

Lexi thinks she can handle it, until Marcus changes the rules and asks for far more than she bargained for. The man is wicked, dangerous, unrelenting. The absolute worst.

He wants to *romance* her.

Sign up for my newsletter and never miss a new release! kyliegilmore.com/newsletter

ALSO BY KYLIE GILMORE

Unleashed Romance <<steamy romcoms with dogs!

Fetching (Book 1)

Dashing (Book 2)

Sporting (Book 3)

Toying (Book 4)

Blazing (Book 5)

Chasing (Book 6)

Daring (Book 7)

Leading (Book 8)

Racing (Book 9)

Loving (Book 10)

The Clover Park Series <<brothers who put family first!

The Opposite of Wild (Book 1)

Daisy Does It All (Book 2)

Bad Taste in Men (Book 3)

Kissing Santa (Book 4)

Restless Harmony (Book 5)

Not My Romeo (Book 6)

Rev Me Up (Book 7)

An Ambitious Engagement (Book 8)

Clutch Player (Book 9)

A Tempting Friendship (Book 10)

Clover Park Bride: Nico and Lily's Wedding

A Valentine's Day Gift (Book 11)

Maggie Meets Her Match (Book 12)

The Clover Park STUDS series <<hawt geeks who unleash into studs!

Almost Over It (Book 1)

Almost Married (Book 2)

Almost Fate (Book 3)

Almost in Love (Book 4)

Almost Romance (Book 5)

Almost Hitched (Book 6)

Happy Endings Book Club Series <<the Campbell family and a romance book club collide!

Hidden Hollywood (Book 1)

Inviting Trouble (Book 2)

So Revealing (Book 3)

Formal Arrangement (Book 4)

Bad Boy Done Wrong (Book 5)

Mess With Me (Book 6)

Resisting Fate (Book 7)

Chance of Romance (Book 8)

Wicked Flirt (Book 9)

An Inconvenient Plan (Book 10)

A Happy Endings Wedding (Book 11)

The Rourkes Series <<swoonworthy princes and kickass princesses!

Royal Catch (Book 1)

Royal Hottie (Book 2)

Royal Darling (Book 3)

Royal Charmer (Book 4)

Royal Player (Book 5)

Royal Shark (Book 6)

Rogue Prince (Book 7)

Rogue Gentleman (Book 8)

Rogue Rascal (Book 9)

Rogue Angel (Book 10)

Rogue Devil (Book 11)

Rogue Beast (Book 12)

**Check out my website for the most up-to-date list of my books:
kyliegilmore.com/books**

ABOUT THE AUTHOR

Kylie Gilmore is the *USA Today* bestselling author of the Unleashed Romance series, the Rourkes series, the Happy Endings Book Club series, the Clover Park series, and the Clover Park STUDS series. She writes humorous romance that makes you laugh, cry, and reach for a cold glass of water.

Kylie lives in New York with her family, two cats, and a nutso dog. When she's not writing, reading hot romance, or dutifully taking notes at writing conferences, you can find her flexing her muscles all the way to the high cabinet for her secret chocolate stash.

Sign up for Kylie's Newsletter and get a FREE book! kyliegilmore.com/newsletter

For text alerts on Kylie's new releases, text KYLIE to the number (888) 707-3025. (US only)

For more fun stuff check out Kylie's website https://www.kyliegilmore.com.

Thanks for reading *Chance of Romance*. I hope you enjoyed it. Would you like to know about new releases? You can sign up for my new release email list at kyliegilmore.com/newsletter. I promise not to clog your inbox! Only new release info, sales, and some fun giveaways.

I love to hear from readers! You can find me at:
kyliegilmore.com
Instagram.com/kyliegilmore
Facebook.com/KylieGilmoreToo
Twitter @KylieGilmoreToo

If you liked Logan and Sabrina's story, please leave a review on your favorite retailer's website or Goodreads. Thank you.